D0442619

MARVEL

GUARDIANS OF THE GALAXY VOL. 2

MARVEL
GUARDIANS OF THE GALAXY VOL. 2

THE JUNIOR NOVEL

ADAPTED BY JIM McCANN
WRITTEN AND DIRECTED BY JAMES GUNN
PRODUCED BY KEVIN FEIGE, P.G.A.

LITTLE, BROWN AND COMPANY
New York   Boston

Little, Brown and Company
Hachette Book Group
1290 Avenue of the Americas, New York, NY 10104
Visit us at lb-kids.com
marvelkids.com

First Edition: April 2017

Little, Brown and Company is a division of Hachette Book Group, Inc.
The Little, Brown name and logo are trademarks of Hachette Book Group, Inc.

The publisher is not responsible for websites (or their content) that are not owned by the publisher.

ISBNs: 978-0-316-27165-3 (pbk.), 978-0-316-27163-9 (hardcover),
978-0-316-31420-6 (ebook), 978-0-316-44029-5 (Scholastic edition)

Printed in the United States of America

LSC-C

10 9 8 7 6 5 4 3 2 1

BONUS

TURN TO PAGE 135
FOR AN EXCLUSIVE
GUARDIANS STORY NOT
SHOWN IN THEATERS!

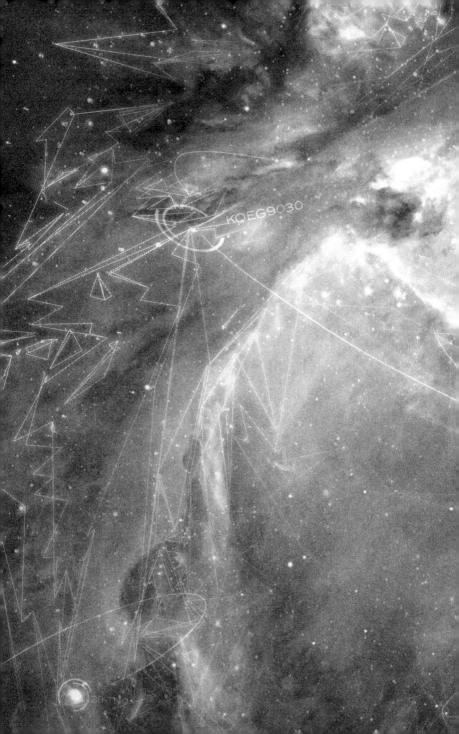

EARTH, 38 YEARS AGO . . .

The hazy summer sun glinted off the hood of an orange-and-teal convertible as it made its way along the winding road, following the Missouri River. It was nearing dusk, and a love song blared from the car stereo as it sped past maple trees, leaving the branches swaying in the wind.

In the passenger seat of the car, Meredith Quill

laughed and sang along as loudly and out of tune as her voice would allow.

"Do-do-do-do-do-do-do…" She echoed the beat of the chorus and began to dance joyfully in her seat.

Next to her, the well-dressed driver, who seemed older than her but oddly ageless—it was actually hard to place—laughed. He reached over and brushed a stray strand of her fine blond hair from her face. She held his hand briefly, then leaned in to sing into it like a microphone. She sang louder until both were overcome with fits of laughter.

Still smiling, the driver turned off the road and parked beside an ice-cream store that stood alone, tucked away in a quiet area far from town.

"Ice cream for dinner? Sounds like a perfect idea to me." Meredith smiled as she hopped out of the car. But the man wasn't headed toward the shop. He walked past the lonely structure toward the edge of the woods behind it. There, he stood, waiting for his companion, his hand outstretched.

An adventure, Meredith thought. Even better than ice cream for dinner. She would go on any adventure.

Taking her hand gently, the man guided Meredith down a steep hillside, snaking their way among the trees. "This way, my river lily." He was corny but charming at the same time.

The two walked farther into the forest. "Where are you taking me?" Meredith asked, barely able to hide the excitement in her voice. The man simply nodded ahead as they continued to walk, finally stopping in front of a particular tree. He waved his arm toward it with a flourish.

Meredith looked at it, puzzled. There was nothing spectacular or even out of the ordinary about this tree. It appeared to be just like all the others in the forest surrounding them—tall, sturdy, beautiful, but still just a tree.

"I don't understand," she began to say. "What does this—?"

The man gently directed her gaze downward, toward the base of the tree, and suddenly, Meredith understood. He hadn't brought her here to look at a tree. What exactly she was looking at, she didn't know, only that it took her breath away.

Nestled in the mossy grass of the forest was an unusual sprout, one that definitely did not belong in these woods. In fact, it didn't seem to belong in any forest or jungle anywhere on Earth. Merely a few inches tall, the plant had a pattern on its limbs that was impossibly complex and uniquely delicate.

"Oh my. It's so beautiful," she whispered, afraid her voice would cause it to collapse.

She glanced up to see the man standing above her. He had been staring at the magnificent plant, but now he looked directly into her eyes. She let herself get lost in his gaze. His eyes were so deep, so unfathomable. It was clear from the way they glinted and sparkled that, much like this sprout, he was not of this planet. If she stared at him long enough, she could almost feel herself being lifted off the earth and flying through space.

"Do you like it?" he asked, shaking her from her trance.

"I do," she said.

"I was afraid its roots wouldn't take to the soil, but it has. Far more quickly than I thought." He looked up, pensive, beyond the canopy of the trees to the sky above. "Soon, it will be everywhere. All across the universe, fulfilling life's one true purpose."

Meredith was taken in by his words. Before she could process them, the man swept Meredith into his arms and stared deeply into her blue eyes. She felt so overcome with emotion that she had to blink away the tears.

"I—I'm not sure what you're talking about," she said, her voice catching, "but I like the way you say it."

The man held her tighter. "No matter what is to come, know this. My heart is yours, Meredith Quill."

Looking up at him, Meredith said in a far-off voice, "I can't believe I fell in love with a space-man." Again, this was a corny couple at their core.

And with that, he kissed her.

CHAPTER 1

Some time later.

An inter-dimensional crack ripped open a section of space momentarily before quickly closing again with a thunderous *clap*.

Parked not far from the tear in the universe was a spaceship called *Milano*, its sleek orange-and-teal design reminiscent of a certain convertible that had raced through the winding roads of a planet on the other side of the galaxy ages ago. Beyond the colors, though, the two vehicles and their passengers couldn't be more different. Mostly.

"That was close. You sure about this, Quill?" asked Rocket as he finished buckling in his space rig and jetted closer to the *Milano*'s PA system, secretly ripping out wires, a sly grin on his furry face.

"It'll be here any minute," answered Peter Quill, the ship's captain. Peter was monitoring a red dot on a homemade device crafted from an old hand-held video game he had carried with him since childhood.

"Which will be its loss," said Gamora, one of the most fearsome assassins in the galaxy. She was wearing a space rig, like Rocket and Quill, as she checked and double-checked a very deadly-looking long-range weapon.

"Is that a rifle?" Quill asked, a little surprised.

"You don't know what a rifle is?" Gamora was equally surprised.

"Of course. I–I just thought your *thing* was a sword," he retorted.

Gamora looked at Quill as if this were his first battle. "We've been hired to stop an inter-dimensional beast from feeding on those batteries' energy, and I'm going to stop it with a *sword*?"

She brushed past him and continued working on her weapon.

"Hey, no need to get all huffy," Quill mumbled. "You're the one being inconsistent here."

But she was right—they had to focus on the battle. He looked around, surveying their mission: guarding the batteries that powered the large conductor towers surrounding them. These power stations were massive, and the batteries were some of the most sought-after sources of energy in the galaxy. Which was exactly why the Guardians of the Galaxy had been hired for this job. The batteries were a source of both pride and power for their clients, helping maintain the beauty and balance of their home world: the Sovereign.

The Sovereign was a magnificent planet, so perfect it was obviously not made by nature. Light glinted off its golden surface, which was made of interlocking orbs rotating in flawless harmony, as it circled a blue sun. The things Peter Quill saw in his travels across the galaxy never ceased to amaze him.

A much louder, much closer inter-dimensional crack quickly shook his wonder.

"I am Groot," said a small young sapling near Quill's boots. Groot had been freed from his pot, but was still far from being his old gigantic and enigmatic self. After their last major adventure, Groot had sacrificed himself for the good of the team... but he was on the mend and starting to get ready to jump back into the fray. He was getting in some practice already, fighting with a small Orloni creature while the rest of the Guardians prepared themselves for a battle on a little bigger scale.

"I agree, pal," Rocket replied.

Gamora looked at Drax. The muscled warrior stood with his blades drawn, looking up at the sky. She pointed to his chest. "Drax, why are you standing there? Suit up with one of Rocket's aero-rigs."

Drax shook his head. "It hurts."

"Hurts?" Gamora had no issues with hers, and she was a quarter his size.

"I have sensitive nipples," he muttered, much to the delight of Rocket, who burst into laughter.

"Aw, poor baby," he teased. "You wanna bottle?"

Drax snorted. "What about *you*? What are you doing over there?"

Rocket held up Quill's tape player, loaded with his Awesome Mix Tape Vol. 2 cassette. "If

I rig this just right, we can listen to tunes while we blow up whatever wants to come through those cracks," he said, going back to work on the ship's PA system. "Then we can do our job and get out of here." Rocket turned to Drax. "You're welcome."

"How is this a priority?" Drax raised his eyebrows and asked incredulously.

"Ask Quill," Rocket said. "He's the one who likes music so much."

Quill got in between the two, trying to defuse the situation. "I gotta go with Drax on this one, Rocket. You could be checking weapons or something other than this."

"Oh, sure, *okayyyy*, Quill," Rocket said, winking at him. Then he went back to work on the PA system.

Quill shook his head. "No, Rocket, I seriously agree with Drax."

"Sure," Rocket said, looking back. "I *know*." He winked again.

"I can clearly see you winking," Drax growled.

Rocket furrowed his brow. "Wait, I thought I was using my left eye."

Any further discussion of the sound system was quickly ended by a massive crack, the largest yet. It shook them all, as though space itself had tilted slightly.

Quill surveyed his team. It was now or never. Time to lead the Guardians of the Galaxy in another epic battle.

"I am Groot." The youthful tree squeaked and jumped up on Rocket, gripping his shoulder.

"Don't worry, pal," Rocket said, pausing his project. "Whatever it is, I'm sure it can't be..." Rocket trailed off as Groot turned him around.

"I am Groot," he said, pointing.

Rocket had crossed paths with some rather nasty

creatures in his day. Usually, he ended up fighting with them, and usually he won. But the pale-pink monstrosity spilling out of the inter-dimensional crack in space was most definitely not like anything he'd ever fought before. This was not going to be an easy win. Fortunately, he had friends. And some music to accompany them.

The creature, known throughout the galaxy as an Abilisk, fed off large energy sources. Every time it opened its mouth and roared, powerful piercing waves escaped through its teeth. This Abilisk was fully grown, almost one hundred feet from mouth to tail. The only thing standing between it and one of the most powerful energy stations in this corner of space were the Guardians of the Galaxy.

It was not a fair fight.

With the press of a button, an upbeat rock song came blaring over the *Milano*'s PA system. Rocket smiled. *Now for the fun part*, he thought. Groot clearly agreed—he had already started dancing.

Quill gave the order. Turning to his fellow Guardians, he said, "Okay, so we've faced bigger. Or not. But we've got this, so let's kick some space-creature butt!" He reached up and turned on the mask-helmet combo that covered his face for extra protection. Fully suited up, he led the charge.

Gamora, Quill, and Rocket used their space rigs to maneuver out of the creature's way, but they couldn't find a way to cause any damage. Drax, with a mighty cry, leaped at it, holding his twin blades.

Dodging and weaving, the Guardians tried finding a weak spot, blasting everywhere, but the beast was just too massive. Diving into another attack, Drax was flung back with a powerful blow, crashing near Groot and destroying the PA system. The music stopped.

"I am Groot," he said angrily, kicking Drax for being so careless. Groot loved that music almost as much as Peter did.

Suddenly, an idea struck. Drax bellowed out to his fellow Guardians, "The beast's hide is too thick. Our weapons do nothing from the outside. I must cut through it from the *inside*!"

Before the other Guardians could register what Drax was planning to do, the warrior let out a glorious roar, charged directly at the Abilisk's mouth, and was swallowed whole.

"Great. Giant Pinkie here just swallowed our teammate. Ideas, Quill?" Rocket asked, firing away.

"What is he thinking?" Quill asked Gamora.

"He thinks he can pierce the beast from the inside of the skin," said Gamora.

"But that doesn't make any sense," Quill replied. "The skin's the same thickness inside and out!"

Gamora gave him a look that said, *Duh!* "I understand that. So what are we going to do?"

Quill was wondering now how they would be able to complete their mission *and* save their short-sighted teammate. He scanned the Abilisk, looking for any sign of damage they may have done. Luck, his secret weapon, paid off when he noticed something on the creature's neck.

"Gamora!" he yelled. "There! On the neck. Not very big, but—"

"I see it," Gamora said coolly. "Get its attention. I will take care of the rest."

Quill jetted up. "Rocket, get it to look up!"

Rocket began his attack while yelling taunts in every language he could think of. The beast roared, and colorful waves of energy flew from its mouth. Rocket dodged just in time, his tail singed.

Attacking from the other side, Quill was shooting

and trying to expose the Abilisk's neck. "Look up here, you big sea monkey!" he shouted.

Suddenly, the creature turned and lunged at Quill.

Gamora aimed, ready to take her shot. Nothing. Her rifle was jammed! Without a second thought, she threw down the weapon and drew her sword. Getting a head start, she leaped onto the creature's neck, plunging her sword into the wound.

The Abilisk gave out a final scream as it crashed onto a platform and died.

Still nursing his bruised tail, Rocket went over and kicked the creature's head. "Ha!" he cried. "Take that!"

Jetting over to Gamora, Quill grinned. "Sword? See? Consistency," he said with a smug smile. "Maybe we shoulda tried that from the start."

Gamora folded her blade, unamused. "You're

questioning my abilities on the field of battle?" she snapped. "Who was it that—"

The sound of the Abilisk stirring interrupted the pair. They both instinctively reached for their weapons. Suddenly, from the open wound, Drax tumbled out. Standing, he raised his arms in victory.

"Ha! See? I have single-handedly vanquished the beast!"

The Guardians turned away, rolling their eyes. Groot picked up a small piece of debris and threw it at him.

"What?" Drax asked as the Guardians jetted back to the *Milano* to clean up before meeting with their client. "You're welcome?"

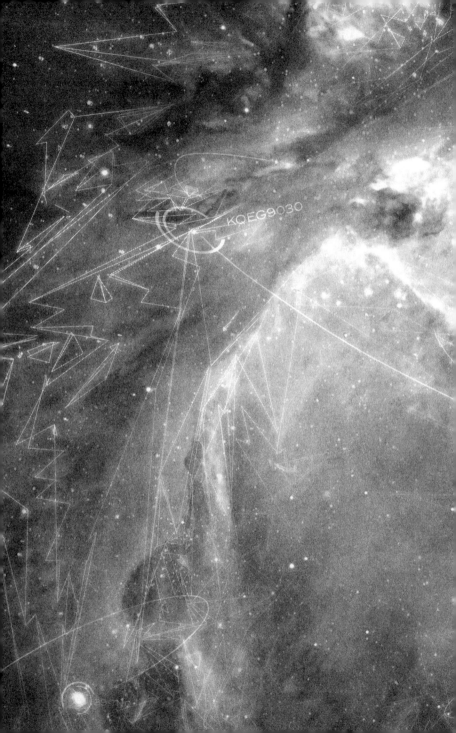

CHAPTER 2

Peter Quill had been to many planets in the years since a mysterious ship had taken him from Earth. Orphaned years ago, he was raised by the blue-skinned Ravager known as Yondu. The Ravagers scoured every inch of the galaxy looking for treasure and lost items (and sometimes stolen items they kept for themselves). Quill had learned the customs of multiple races and the reputations of countless more. This knowledge—and his own personal charm, he liked to think—kept him alive, even after he'd left the Ravagers.

It was also what would keep his team alive here on the Sovereign planet. If they followed his lead.

"Look, guys. Trust me on this. Be extra careful of what you say around these guys," Quill warned.

"Why are you looking at me?" Rocket said defensively. "It's not like I'm gonna get us killed or anything."

"Actually, the Sovereign are easily offended, and the punishment is death," Peter corrected him.

Drax snorted. "Sounds judgmental for a bunch of golden morons."

Peter shushed the warrior and looked around quickly to see if anyone had heard him. "See," he said, "*that's* the kind of thing you might want to keep to yourself."

"I'll hold my tongue," Gamora said with an icy tone, "as long as they deliver what was promised."

"If they hold such standards, they should be grateful to us, after we defended their . . . what were they called again?" Drax asked as they made their way to the temple.

"Anulax batteries," Quill answered.

"Harbulary batteries," Drax repeated . . . sort of.

"Okay, that's nothing like what I said. Important thing is, they're worth thousands of units apiece." Peter was beginning to think he should have come alone on this part of the mission. "New plan," he said. "Let me do all the talking."

The Sovereign citizens were all gold-skinned and impeccably dressed in the finest clothes in the galaxy. They walked with grace, their movements like a dance, their feet seeming to barely touch the ground. The jewels that adorned the citizens complemented them as if specifically made for him or her.

The Guardians entered the main chamber of the high priestess, Ayesha, and even Rocket's breath caught in his throat. Of all the citizens they had seen so far, she was the closest thing to perfection. The chambermaids and servants surrounding her paled in comparison.

She stood to greet them, and Quill awkwardly offered a half bow.

"High Priestess Ayesha. You're looking very, uh, nice today," he stammered.

" 'Nice'?" The tone of her voice was both cool and questioning.

"That is, I mean, um, *better* than nice? Very... pretty?" Quill was at a loss for words.

Ayesha looked down on him from her raised perch, and a slight smirk flickered across her face.

"Every Sovereign citizen is born exactly as designed

by the community: impeccable, both physically and mentally," she said, an air of pride surrounding her.

"Sounds complicated, but you seem to be doing good so far," Quill said, not sure if she was waiting for an answer.

"We control the DNA of our progeny, germinating them in birthing pods," Ayesha continued.

"Pretty much not my kind of thing," he said. A sideways glance at Gamora staring at him stopped Quill mid-sentence.

Gamora gave an exasperated sigh and said, "Oh please," before stepping in front of Peter and addressing Ayesha. "Your people promised something in trade for our services. Bring it and we shall gladly be on our way."

Ayesha turned her gaze to the green-skinned woman, her head tilting in near admiration at Gamora's boldness. Looking to her guards, she nodded. A few seconds later, two guards returned with a woman, a hood covering her head, her wrists shackled together. Pushing her to her knees, one of the guards ripped off the hood, revealing the deadly assassin Nebula!

It took a moment for her eyes to adjust to her surroundings. Looking behind her, she saw the high priestess's dispassionate gaze. In front of her, she saw a group of well-armed warriors. She had traded one set of captors for another. She recognized the Guardians of the Galaxy—making note of one in particular who was glaring fiercely at her. She curled her lips and stared back at Gamora.

"Family reunion. *Yaaaay*," Peter muttered.

"I understand she is your sister," Ayesha stated to Gamora, who was approaching Nebula.

Grabbing Nebula roughly and lifting her to her feet, Gamora sneered. "She's worth no more to me than the bounty due for her on Xandar." She barely acknowledged her sister. Nebula did her best to do the same.

Ayesha waved off the sisters, seeming to be glad to be rid of something so beneath her. "Our soldiers apprehended her attempting to steal some Anulax batteries. Do with her as you please."

As the Guardians began to file out of the chamber, Quill made another awkward bow. "Thank you, High Priestess Ayesha," he said, and turned to go as well.

"Mr. Quill." Ayesha's voice rang out, stopping him. "What is your heritage?"

Peter seemed taken aback by the question. "My mother is from Earth," he said.

"And your father?" Ayesha pressed.

Quill paused. "He's...not from Missouri," he said. "That's all I really know." He shifted his feet from side to side uncomfortably. This was not a topic he liked to dwell on, much less talk about with Sovereign priestesses.

Ayesha stared at him intently, as if she were studying him, able to see his very DNA. Her face turned into a sneer of near disgust. "I see it within you, your unorthodox genealogy," she said. "A hybrid that seems particularly...reckless."

Quill felt on his face the sting of her words. His blood began to boil, but he remembered his earlier warning to his team about insulting the Sovereign.

Quill stomped past Rocket, who followed him out of the chamber, but not before turning to address the high priestess. "You know, they told me you people were a bunch of jerks," Rocket said casually. "But that isn't true at all."

The entire team froze. Rocket winked at Drax before he realized: "Oh man, I'm using the wrong eye again, aren't I?" Turning back to Ayesha, he offered an apology in his own way. "I'm sorry," he said. "That was meant to be behind your back."

Ayesha stared at them for a long moment and then, with the slightest gesture, dismissed them with a curt wave of her hand. Quill and Gamora quickly hurried out with Nebula, followed closely by Rocket and Drax.

"Count yourself blessed they didn't kill you," said the big warrior.

"Heh, that's nothing, pal," Rocket replied with a mischievous grin. "We got the last laugh." He rolled up his sleeve to reveal five stolen Anulax batteries!

Drax's eyes widened, and he began to laugh, but Rocket hushed him as he returned his contraband to its hiding spot.

Back at the Sovereign space dock, the Guardians boarded the *Milano*, nestled among the Sovereign's fleet of sleek capsule-shaped ships. Like everything about the Sovereign, the ships looked as though they were meant to slice through space with exact precision. Rows and rows of them lined the dock.

With everyone on board, Rocket guided the *Milano* away from the golden planet just as the blue sun began to set.

CHAPTER 3

Usually the music from the Awesome Mix Tape Vol. 2 was enough to brighten Peter Quill's mood. Or at least take his mind off whatever might be bothering him. But as the *Milano* flew out of the Sovereign's orbit, not even the bouncy, up-tempo song playing from the repaired PA system's speaker could lift his spirits.

Quill seemed to be in a wrestling match with his

jacket as he tried to shake it off. Finally freed, he threw it to the ground as Gamora passed. "You all right?" she asked. "Or did the jacket offend you and you've now taken up the Sovereign customs?"

"The Sovereign?" Quill spat the words in disgust as he flopped into a seat on the flight deck.

"That high priestess did seem to overstep her bounds," Gamora reflected.

"Right?" Quill sat up, his face momentarily flushed. "That stuff about 'reckless hybrid.' Hey, lady, people who live in glass houses shouldn't throw stones." He leaned back in his seat. "And that stuff about my father?" he continued. "Who does she think she is?"

Gamora put her hand on his arm. "I know you're sensitive about that."

"I'm not sensitive about it," Peter said, a little too forcefully to cover the lie. "I just don't know who he is."

Gamora nodded at him. Being the adopted daughter of the genocidal mad titan Thanos, she knew what it was like to have a complicated relationship with your father.

Registering the touch of Gamora's hand on his arm, Quill suddenly recalled the scene from earlier. "Oh man, Gamora," he said awkwardly. "Sorry if it looked like I was flirting with her back there. I wasn't. I just started talking—"

Gamora removed her hand from Peter's arm. "I don't care if you were flirting," she said, her tone unreadable.

Peter leaned in, a playful glint in his eye. "See, I think you do care," he insisted. "That's why I'm apologizing."

Gamora got up and moved toward the back of the ship, grabbing Nebula by the chains along the way.

"Still sorry!" Quill called after her. He watched

her leave and then leaned back, smiling. His mind returned to the time when he'd introduced Gamora to music on Knowhere. The balcony, the starlight. Even thinking of the battle earlier, when she used her sword to slay the Abilisk with no hesitation, made his smile grow into a goofy grin. The way she used her sword, it seemed so natural. He could still feel her hand on his arm. It felt as if—

"Gamora is not the one for you, Quill."

Drax, standing over him, abruptly interrupted Quill's thoughts.

"I wasn't...She and I...We're not—" Quill stammered.

"You were staring at her, were you not?" Drax asked.

"I wasn't staring," Quill said defensively.

"There are two types of beings in the universe," Drax continued, ignoring him, "those who dance and those who do not."

"Uh-huh." Quill wasn't sure where Drax was going with this, which wasn't too unusual with Drax.

Drax looked out the window, gazing at the stars. "I first met my beloved at a war rally. Everyone in the village flailed about, their arms and legs in every direction. *Dancing.* Except one woman. My Ovette. I knew immediately she was the one."

"Because your thing is being a buzzkill?" Quill asked, genuinely confused.

"The most melodic song in the world could be playing and she wouldn't even tap her foot," Drax answered plainly. "She wouldn't move a muscle. She was so still among so many people dancing about, one might assume she was dead." Drax smiled at the thought.

"Well, yeah, I can see how that's pretty—" Quill lied as best he could.

"It would make my heart race—" Drax continued, completely wrapped up in the memory.

"Okay," Quill quickly interrupted, waving his arms. "Fascinating. Beautiful. Love story for the ages. I don't need to know the rest. I get your point. I'm a dancer and Gamora is not."

Drax turned back to Quill, placed his hands on his shoulders, and smiled, saying, "You just need to find a woman who is pathetic. Like you."

The big warrior squeezed Quill's shoulders, then let go and left.

"Great talk. Really," Quill called after him. "Next time I need a pick-me-up, I know where to go. Thanks!" Shaking his head, he snuck a glance down the ship toward Gamora and Nebula.

In the back of the *Milano*, Gamora did not show her sister any kindness as she secured her to the wall. For a moment, both sisters refused to look at each other. Nebula's eyes rested on a bowl of fruit.

"I am hungry," she said. "Hand me some of that yaro root." It was more a demand than a request.

"No. It is not ripe yet," Gamora answered flatly. "Also, I can't stand you."

"You can't stand *me*?!" Nebula snapped furiously. "You left me there—"

"You flew away. Your choice," Gamora interrupted.

"Left me there," Nebula continued, ignoring her sister, "while you stole that stone for yourself. Yes, I'm in these chains because I tried to steal, yet here you stand, a 'hero'—some sort of 'Garden of the Galaxy'!"

"Some sort of what?" Gamora asked, not sure what her sister had just said. She and Nebula stared at each other, both confused. Suddenly, it dawned on Gamora. "Oh, '*Guardians* of the Galaxy.'"

"Whatever," Nebula said, trying to hide her ignorance.

"Why would we be the 'Gardens of the Galaxy'?" Gamora asked, bewildered.

Nebula shrugged. "You have a tree and a furry creature," she said. "I don't know. I thought it was stupid anyway."

"That it would be," Gamora agreed.

"It's still wordy," Nebula said, trying to provoke her sister.

Gamora refused to take the bait and said, "I wasn't the one who thought of it."

Suddenly, Nebula lunged at Gamora, her face stopping mere inches away from her sister's. Gamora didn't blink, knowing the bonds that held Nebula were tight enough to restrain Drax. There was a fire in Nebula's eyes.

"Your name doesn't matter," Nebula spat. "I'll be free of these shackles soon enough, and when I am, I'll kill you. I swear it."

Gamora stared into her sister's eyes, emotionless. "No," she calmly replied. "You'll live out your days in a prison on Xandar, wishing you could."

The sisters stood staring at each other in silence for a few moments, until the blaring sound of the ship's alarms interrupted their standoff. The lights above them began to flash. Gamora ran to the stairs and quickly ascended to the flight deck. Drax joined her as the two ran toward the cockpit, where Rocket and Quill were already seated.

"Why the alarms?" she asked.

Rocket pointed to the monitor. Gamora didn't flinch as Quill exclaimed, "Because we have an armed Sovereign fleet on our tail!"

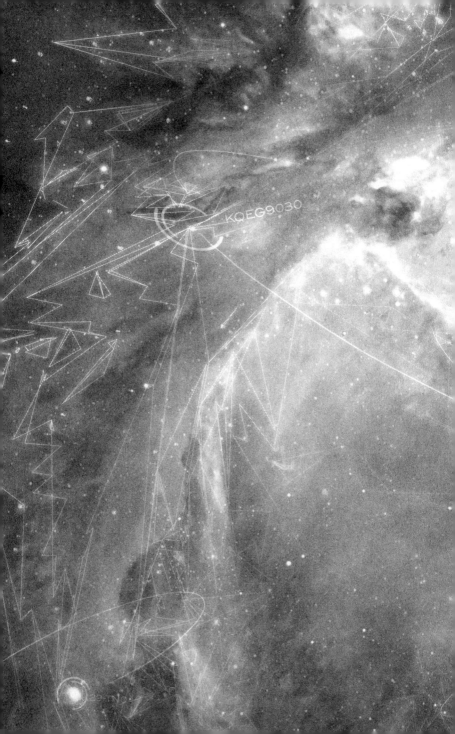

CHAPTER 4

The Sovereign fleet had a reputation throughout the galaxy for its precision, speed, and cunning. The capsule-shaped golden omnicraft were capped on both ends by deadly blasters. Like all Sovereign citizens, their pilots were designed at birth to be nothing short of perfect. The sight of nearly two dozen ships closing in would send anyone into a panic. The crew of the *Milano* was no exception.

"This is so not good," Quill said, wiping sweat off his brow and trying to think his way out of a firefight with the golden fleet.

"Why are they targeting us?" Gamora asked. "We completed our mission!" She was baffled as the fleet slowly approached.

"Probably because Rocket stole some of their batteries," Drax stated casually.

Rocket whipped his furry head around and shot him a betrayed look. "Dude!"

"Oh. Right. He didn't steal those. I don't know why they are after us. What a mystery this is." Too late, Drax tried to cover.

Quill and Gamora stared at Rocket, both ready to explode with anger. On the monitors, the Sovereign fleet was close enough now to see images of the pilots' faces, jaws set in determination to destroy those who had dared commit such a crime.

Rocket pointed at a screen and shouted, "Incoming!"

Quill steered the ship, barely dodging the blast from the Sovereign omnicraft.

"There's no turning back now." Gamora sighed.

"What were you thinking?" Quill yelled at Rocket, jerkily evading another blast.

Rocket shrugged. "Dude, they were really easy to steal," he explained.

"That's your defense?" Gamora asked, amazed by his audacity. "I should shackle you with Nebula below the deck."

Rocket looked at them as if they were the ones who didn't get it. "Come on," he pleaded. "You saw how that high priestess talked down to us! Especially you, Quill. I'm teaching her a lesson!"

Quill smacked his forehead. "Oh! I didn't realize your motivation was altruism and this was all just Rocket's Good Deed of the Day," he said with exaggerated gratitude. "Such a shame the Sovereign didn't realize it, either, and are now trying to kill us. My bad."

Rocket sat back, his furry arms crossed, and said, "Exactly."

"I was being sarcastic!" Quill shouted.

"Oh no, you tricked me! You're supposed to use your sarcastic voice! Now I look foolish!" Rocket snapped back, equally sarcastic.

Drax laughed at Rocket as the creature got more and more flustered.

"Shut up, Drax!" Quill shouted. "You knew about this. You're just as guilty that we're in this mess." Quill fumed, swerving to avoid another Sovereign blast.

Gamora slammed her hand against the cockpit. "Can everyone just put the bickering on hold until after we survive the massive space battle?" she scolded through gritted teeth.

Rocket and Quill stared at each other for a moment. Rocket cocked his eyebrow, nodding back at Gamora. "Wowza," he said. "Someone woke up on the wrong side of the bed this morning."

Quill's eyebrows cinched together. He was not amused. "Do *not* try to bro down with me right now, dude," he said, his voice strained. "All I want to do is punch you in the face."

"Real nice," Rocket protested, throwing his hands in the air. "Resorting to violence."

"Shut. Up!" Quill hissed. He looked at the monitors and steered away from another omnicraft blast.

"For such a commanding and fearsome presence, these ships sure seem to miss rather often," Gamora mused.

"Thanks for the flying credit," Quill said, slightly offended.

"My point is that these seem to be warning shots,"

Gamora explained. "If they wanted us dead by now, I feel they would have put more of an effort into it."

"Well, you're about to get to test that theory," Quill said, pointing ahead as another battalion of Sovereign omnicraft appeared in front of them. "More incoming!"

"Good!" Rocket exclaimed, aiming the *Milano*'s guns at the approaching omnicraft. "I wanna fry some guys!" Rocket began firing the ship's guns at the oncoming Sovereign fleet.

The fleet broke formation, deftly avoiding the barrage of gunfire from the *Milano*. The omnicraft pitched and rolled, their sleek capsule shapes dancing through space between the blasts. A video monitor in the center of each capsule displayed a Sovereign pilot, determination and focus bred into their DNA. The superiority of the pilots' skills was apparent as their eyes never left their target, despite the rapid-fire shots Rocket was unleashing.

One laser beam flew from the *Milano*'s cannon and sped through space, aimed directly at a Sovereign omnicraft. The pilot saw it and hesitated slightly. That was his downfall. As the beam collided with the ship, his face on the monitor tensed in anger and surprise.

Rocket cheered. "Nailed ya, sucker! One dead, now who's next?"

Gamora looked closer at the ships, pointing to the center where the video monitors were. "No one," she said. "Those faces. They're not in the ships. Those ships are remotely piloted."

"Then I can blow 'em all outta the sky," Rocket said with a grin.

Dodging more Sovereign warning blasts, Quill wondered aloud, "If they're not in there, then where are the pilots?"

Back on the Sovereign planet near the flight deck was a large control bay. Inside were rows upon rows of pods, each containing a Sovereign pilot staring at a video monitor. They maneuvered flight controls with targeting locks and missile-launching buttons as if they were actually inside the omnicraft, yet they safely controlled each ship from their own pod.

On one monitor, a cannon blast from the *Milano* was headed straight for the remote ship. The pilot froze—suddenly, her screen turned to static. She yelled in frustration at her failure. Her cursing cut off abruptly as she looked up at the observation deck. Her commanding officer was giving her a disapproving look; however, it was the figure approaching him that forced her into a silent bow.

High Priestess Ayesha strode gracefully to the

admiral of her fleet, a displeased look clearly etched on her usually serene face. "What is the delay, Admiral?" she said impatiently.

The admiral was hesitant. "High Priestess, if we destroy their craft, we run the risk of destroying the batteries," he explained. "As you know, they are extraordinarily combustible and could, in turn, destroy our entire fleet."

Ayesha waved her hand, cutting off further discussion. Turning to the admiral, her jaw set, she drew to her full height and addressed him: "We have thousands of batteries and thousands of ships. Our concern is avenging their slight against our people. We hire them and they steal from us? The sheer audacity alone is heresy of the highest order."

"Y-yes, High Priestess," the admiral stuttered in the face of her fury.

"Now give the command," Ayesha ordered as she took a step back, her eyes never leaving his.

The admiral bowed after a moment and moved to the communication station. Flipping a switch so all pilots could hear him, he spoke into the comm. "All command modules..."

In space, the Guardians watched the video monitors of the Sovereign omnicraft showing the pilots tilting their heads slightly, awaiting their new orders.

The admiral hesitated slightly as he composed himself enough to speak the words with authority:

"Fire with intent to kill."

CHAPTER 5

Rocket yelled as he swiveled around the ship's gun, blasting at everything in sight.

"I am Groot," said the young sapling in a calming tone.

"Yeah, yeah, pal, I know, I know. These are remotes, not real pilots, blah blah blah." Rocket grinned over at his friend and winked. "That's what makes this even better—"

"I suggest less talking and more firing," Drax interrupted angrily. "Their fleet does not seem to be engaging in banter."

Gamora glanced out the window. She tried her best not to let panic creep into her voice as she warned, "The entire fleet just opened fire."

"Tell me something I don't know!" yelled Quill, concentrating on dodging the sudden barrage of firepower.

"Guess they're done warning us," Rocket said with a gulp as he returned fire.

"You!" Quill snapped at Rocket, still angry about the swiped batteries. "Not another word until—" His words were cut off as the *Milano* suddenly jolted harshly to the left. Alarms blared, and the emergency systems went into overdrive.

"That does not bode well," Drax said, stating the obvious.

"You think?" snapped Gamora.

"We've just lost a good portion of our right wing," Quill informed the team.

"There is no way we can continue to outmaneuver them. No offense," said Gamora, surveying the number of ships now firing on them.

"For once, none taken," Quill muttered. Even he knew he couldn't outfly this many ships, and they were most definitely outgunned. "Quick, what's the closest habitable planet?"

Gamora stood at a monitor, her fingers dancing across a keyboard, her eyes scanning the planets as they zoomed across the screen. Drax looked over her shoulder.

"There?" Drax pointed.

"He said *habitable*," Gamora said, shoving his hand out of the way.

Drax grunted and stepped away in a huff. He could tell when his help wasn't appreciated.

"Got one," Gamora called out. "It's called Berhert."

"Sounds lovely. How many clicks?" Quill pressed, his voice getting tenser.

"Only one," Gamora answered, though her voice sounded unconvincing.

"What's the catch?" Quill asked, noting her tone.

"The access point is through that quantum asteroid field to our left," Gamora replied, delivering the bad news.

Quill looked out and saw what she was referring to. A quantum asteroid field was unlike a normal collection of rock clusters flying through space. That would have been difficult enough to fly through. This was a huge field of glowing asteroids that swirled about in random patterns, comprised of individual asteroids that would disappear, only to emerge again seconds later a few yards away. There was no rhyme or reason to the way a quantum asteroid field operated, making it nearly impossible to navigate.

With one deft motion, Quill turned the *Milano* to the left and headed straight for the chaotic field.

Drax looked at him, equal parts dubious and impressed. "I am amazed, Quill," he said. "To make it through that, you'd have to be the greatest pilot in the universe."

Without taking his eyes off the quantum field, Peter smirked and said, "Lucky for us—"

"I am!" Rocket exclaimed, interrupting Peter.

With a swift gesture, Rocket flipped the pilot control switch so he was now in charge of navigating the ship.

"Give that back!" Quill shouted. "I thought you were having fun with the 'Die! Die! Die!'" He reached for the pilot control switch.

Rocket swatted away his hand. "Your turn to shoot now," he said. "This looks like way more fun."

The *Milano* dove deeper into the quantum asteroid field. Glowing, swirling stones appeared and disappeared in front of them. Rocket veered to the right just as a cluster appeared where the ship had been moments ago. Gamora stifled a gasp. Groot hid under a chair. Drax watched with a grin on his face at the thought of such a glorious escape from certain death.

Behind them, the Sovereign fleet followed into the field. While they were bred to be perfect pilots, recklessness was not in their genetic makeup. The idea of such behavior was something most pilots were unable to grasp. Those pilots' omnicraft were almost immediately pulverized as the quantum stones crashed into their ships.

On the Sovereign planet, pod after pod saw their monitors go dark as their ships were destroyed in the asteroid field. The pilots climbed out, some hanging their heads in shame, others clearly shaken, while many pounded their now-useless pods in anger. None, however, dared look up to the observation deck.

Ayesha watched as one after another of her pilots failed her. It was not a sight to which she was accustomed, and it angered her. She gripped the railing, leaning in, her eyes narrowing as the *Milano* slipped away from her fleet.

Back in the asteroid field, a fight raged within the *Milano* for control of the ship. While Rocket concentrated on avoiding an approaching cluster, Quill reached for the switch and flipped it so he was once again piloting. He dove under the cluster at the last second.

"What are you doing?" Rocket asked with a look of exhasperation.

"I've been flying this rig since I was ten years old!" Quill retorted, expertly dodging an asteroid that had suddenly appeared in front of them.

"Well, I was cybernetically engineered to pilot a spacecraft! Beat that, Earthboy!" Rocket taunted, flipping the control back to himself, then quickly jerking the ship away from an asteroid that nearly collided with them head-on.

"You were cybernetically engineered to be a pain in the butt!" Quill sniped. He took back control and flew over a particularly large glowing rock.

Gamora slammed her hand between the two of them. "Stop it!" she yelled. "Before you get us all killed."

Rocket sat back, glaring at her.

Gamora sighed.

Rocket grinned, seeing his opportunity to reach the newly unprotected switch. "Gotcha," he yelled triumphantly.

"I *will* shave you," Quill threatened.

At this, Drax laughed loudly. Gamora shot him a look. "We're about to die and this is what we're discussing?" she said.

Drax shrugged.

"Enough!" Gamora shouted, fed up.

The *Milano* continued to dodge and weave erratically through the quantum asteroid field as Rocket and Quill jockeyed for control.

"Give it!" Quill yelled.

"Try shooting at some of those ships still following us!" Rocket replied.

Behind them, the Sovereign omnicraft continued their pursuit, but the constantly shifting asteroids were slowly thinning their numbers.

Back on the observation deck, Ayesha was growing impatient. She turned to the admiral. "This failure is unacceptable," she admonished.

"Respectfully, High Priestess, we couldn't have prepared for a scenario where they would actually attempt such an insane maneuver," the admiral replied. "I doubt they are even aware of the explosive damage their stolen cargo is capable of. If they were, no one in their right mind would have—"

The withering look from Ayesha silenced the

admiral. "I did not ask for an assessment of the hybrid and his crew's mind-set," she hissed. "It is time to stop making excuses and start providing successful alternatives."

"Yes, High Priestess," the admiral answered, quickly moving away to study a map of the surrounding star field on one monitor and the progress of his remaining pilots on another.

Ayesha stared at the remaining pilots in their pods who were doing everything they could just to maneuver through the quantum asteroids, much less stay hot on the trail of the *Milano*.

"We're nearing the edge of the field," Gamora announced, relief starting to ease into her voice. "And only a handful of Sovereign ships remain."

"Wonderful. Now let me get us out of the homestretch," Quill said, reaching for the controls.

"No way! I did most of the flying. Who says you get to take the credit at the end?" Rocket yelled, reaching for the control at the same time.

Both pilots had their hands on the switch for a moment, and in that moment neither had their eyes on the ship's monitor. Before Gamora could shout a warning, a large asteroid *slammed* into the rear of the *Milano*, shaking the entire craft.

"We're hit!" Rocket screamed over the deafening alarms.

"Really?! What was your first clue, genius?" Quill yelled back. "Where?"

Gamora surveyed the monitors. "Lower rear section," she said, suddenly growing pale.

"What's down there?" Quill asked as the ship began to pitch about.

"Nebula," Gamora replied, already racing back to reach her sister, but she was slammed against a wall before she could make it to the stairwell.

At the back of the *Milano*, a large chunk of the ship had been ripped away by the collision with the asteroid. Boxes of gear and other cargo that wasn't fastened down were being sucked into the cold vacuum of space.

Nebula floated sideways, her body pulled toward the gaping hole. Her chains, shackled against the far wall, held her in place, keeping her inside the craft. But as the hole began to tear wider, sucking more and more atmosphere and cargo from the ship, Nebula was slowly exposed to the creeping space. Her cries for help went unheard as her face and body began to cover over with frost.

CHAPTER 6

The *Milano* was in chaos! The hole grew bigger and bigger as more things went crashing toward the vast emptiness of space. Cargo, supplies, and weapons were being rapidly sucked closer to the gaping hole.

"I am Groot!" shouted the young sapling, swept up in a current of air.

"Hold on, buddy!" Peter Quill switched on his Star-Lord mask and frantically reached out toward

Groot, who put out a branch in turn, continuing to extend it several inches until both branch and arm clasped. Star-Lord gave a tug and pulled Groot back to safety.

"I am Groot," he said, relieved.

"Yeah, yeah you are," Star-Lord replied, "but we're not out of this yet." He spotted a flashing button above him. Looking back down at Groot, he said, "Think I can get a lift?"

Groot smiled. Wrapping his branches around Star-Lord's boots, he helped lift him almost a foot in the air.

Now face-to-face with the blinking button, Star-Lord slammed his hand against it. Suddenly, a blue energy shield appeared at the back of the ship, extending to cover the hole. Nebula fell back to the floor with a *thud*.

Star-Lord turned to the other Guardians and

slid off his mask. "See? Backup shields," he said with swagger. Gamora glared at him.

From the back of the ship, a thawing Nebula's voice yelled, "Idiots!"

"Can we not for about five minutes? All that space vacuuming—" Rocket gave his head a vigorous shake, only to be interrupted by Drax laughing.

Pointing at Rocket, Drax said, "You look like an electrified Orloni!"

Rocket looked at his reflection in the window. It was true. All his fur was standing on end after being whipped about by air currents.

Rocket scowled. "Well, that's what you get when Quill is flying," he muttered.

Gamora wasn't paying any attention to him. Looking out the window, she opened her mouth in alarm. "Look—there's another one!"

"Another what?" Quill asked, running back to

the cockpit. "Abilisk? Asteroid? Hole in the ship? I need specifics."

"Sovereign ship. And it's closing in fast," Gamora said grimly.

"A fine warrior, indeed. I would like to meet this pod pilot," Drax said, nodding, impressed.

"Meet him? He's trying to *kill* us," Rocket explained.

"A small matter. Once that is settled, we shall meet," Drax said, crossing his arms, ending any further conversation.

Suddenly, a blast from the Sovereign ship grazed the *Milano*, and all the lights flickered before going completely dark. Gamora punched a series of codes into the console before slamming her fist on the metal.

"Our weapons are down!" she exclaimed.

"Now we shall see what this pod pilot can do," Drax said, disappearing toward the back of the ship with an excited look.

"Gamora, how far off did our detour take us?" Quill asked.

"We're twenty clicks away from the jump point," she replied.

Another blast rocked the ship, this one taking out the left wing. Rocket and Quill looked at each other, both thinking the same thing: *Okay, hotshot, get us out of this one!* But neither had any idea what to do next.

Out of the corner of his eye, Quill saw Drax descending into the hull of the ship. "Oh great. We have our first deserter...." he muttered.

"He's gaining on us," Rocket reported. "What do we do without weapons? Should I just start throwing yaro root and Drax poop at him?"

"I'm thinking!" Quill said, running rapidly out of options.

"Oh. Quill's thinking. We're dead for sure," Rocket quipped.

In the back of the ship, Nebula watched Drax approach.

"I'm fine, thanks. Glad someone finally came to check on me," she said bitterly.

"Nebula, I did not know you were here," Drax replied, just remembering the prisoner they had on board. "I am glad to see you alive." He brushed past her before she could say another word, her jaw hanging open in disbelief that no one had thought to see if she'd been sucked into space.

She watched Drax grab a cable from the wall and hook it to a loop on his belt. "Where are you going?" she demanded.

Drax smiled and said, "To meet a worthy foe."

Over in the Sovereign pilot bay, some of the defeated Sovereign had gathered next to the lone pilot left chasing the *Milano*, cheering him on. Above, on the observation deck, High Priestess Ayesha motioned to the admiral. "That pilot," she said, pointing down to where everyone was gathered. "Tell me more about him."

"H-his name is Zylak," the admiral stuttered. "Top of his class. Laser focus. Killer instinct. Had to be disciplined once for being too aggressive."

Ayesha smiled. "Unleash him," she commanded.

Zylak heard the admiral's command in his comm unit, and his lips curled into a vicious sneer. "Roger that," he replied. "Tell Her Highness I live to serve at her pleasure." He leaned forward and banked his Sovereign pod to the right, unleashing a barrage of laser blasts on the weaponless *Milano*. He had been impressed by the skills of the pilot in the asteroid field, even though his evasion tactics had seemed erratic. Whoever was flying was gifted; there was no denying that. It was a shame he had to destroy the ship, but its passengers had to pay for their crimes against the Sovereign.

Another stream of lasers hurtled toward the *Milano*. One found its mark on the left wing, blowing it apart on impact. Inside, each Guardian grabbed on to the closest secure thing they could find as the *Milano* went spinning into a brief spiral.

"Wingless *and* weaponless. Anyone got any ideas?" Rocket asked.

"I am Groot?" the little tree suggested.

Rocket grinned at Groot's suggestion. "Sorry, pal," he said, "I don't think even Drax—"

In the back of the ship, Drax found a slot in the wall labeled SPACE SUITS FOR EMERGENCY. Under that, in Rocket's scribbled writing, were the words "OR FOR FUN." He reached into the slot and pulled out a disc, which he slapped on the middle of his chest. Immediately, his entire body was covered by a shimmering gel-like sheath. His eyes lit up, and he grinned widely.

In the Sovereign pilot bay, Zylak had a similar glint in his eye as he readied himself for another pass. He unleashed a targeted blast, clipping the topside of the *Milano*. At this point, he was toying with them. Over his comm unit, he could hear his fellow pilots cheering him on. *Okay*, he thought, *enough fun: Time to execute the thieves.* He directed his Sovereign pod up and around, positioning for his final approach.

On the flight deck of the *Milano*, Gamora eyed the radar display nervously. "Fifteen clicks," she said.

"Looks like he's coming around again," Rocket

replied. "Hey, Drax, maybe you could throw your blades—" He stopped short and looked around. "Has anyone seen Drax?" he asked.

Meanwhile, wearing his shimmering space suit, Drax reached into another box bolted to the wall of the ship. Inside was a large, lethal-looking rifle.

"Do not even think of stealing. I do not like thieves," Drax said bluntly.

"*Umm*, have you looked at the people you hang out with?" Nebula asked, pointing toward the flight deck.

Drax paused, then grunted. "They are exceptions," he said. "Now, good-bye."

"'Good-bye'?" Nebula repeated before watching in shock as Drax exited through the backup shield, his own space suit momentarily merging with it before he floated out into space with his rifle.

On the flight deck, Gamora's eyes widened as she saw an image on her console. "I think I found

Drax," she said, pointing out the side window at the huge warrior, who had his rifle aimed squarely at the approaching Sovereign.

Quill slowly banged his head against the wall. "This cannot end well," he groaned. "Do other people have to deal with this level of crazy?"

On his screen, Zylak was shocked to see a small gray object floating behind his target, connected by some kind of cable. As he got a closer look, he saw it had arms and legs. Scanning his data files, he realized it was one of the perpetrators: the Guardian they called Drax. Zylak chuckled. What a great opportunity for some target practice. Destroying the ship could wait a few more moments. He narrowed his targeting lasers on Drax and pulled the trigger.

The *Milano* suddenly jerked to the side, pulling the big warrior behind it. He barely seemed to notice how close he had come to being blown to pieces. Lifting his rifle, he took aim at the Sovereign ship and pulled the trigger.

He smiled.

The laser from Drax's rifle found its mark. Back in the Sovereign pilot bay, Zylak screamed as his ship blew up. He threw down his controls in defeat, and saw High Priestess Ayesha watching from above. Her face was not happy. Zylak knelt before her, but when he looked up again, she was gone.

"Five clicks!" Gamora exclaimed. They were about to make the jump.

"Perfect timing." Drax's voice boomed as he reappeared on the flight deck. "Once again, I have single-handedly destroyed our foe!"

Quill considered correcting Drax, then thought better of it. "Nice shot, big guy. All right, now it's time to...Oh no!"

Looking ahead out the window, Quill felt his

excitement immediately turn to despair. Dozens of Sovereign ships flew into formation between the *Milano* and the jump point.

On the Sovereign flight deck, Ayesha smiled faintly at the admiral. "You have redeemed yourself," she said flatly. "Nicely done, Admiral."

Back on the *Milano*, Rocket looked at the Sovereign ships in disbelief. "How did they do that?" he asked, already grabbing his gun out of its holster. He was ready to go down fighting.

"They must have flown around the asteroid field," Quill answered. "Kind of like the tortoise and the hare thing."

Drax was confused. "Is Rocket the hare?" he asked.

"I'd teach you all about parables if we weren't about to die, Drax," Quill said.

"I am Groot." The other Guardians watched as Groot reached past them and tapped on a side window, directing their view to the space between the *Milano* and the Sovereign fleet: A sleek, oval-shaped floating ship had appeared seemingly out of nowhere.

"Yeah." Rocket nodded. "I've never seen a ship like that before, either. Guys, you gotta see—"

Suddenly, a blinding burst of light cut off what Rocket was about to say. When the Guardians could see again, the entire Sovereign fleet was gone, apparently vaporized by the white light that appeared to have emanated from the strange floating vessel.

On the Sovereign flight deck, all was silent as the admiral delivered to Ayesha the news of the fleet's destruction. She merely stood in place for several moments. The admiral gulped. After a long pause, Ayesha turned to the admiral.

"Who did this?" she asked, her voice growing louder with every word.

The admiral bowed his head helplessly. Ayesha looked at the hundreds of now-useless pilots standing below her, their heads also hung in shame. Without acknowledging them any further, she turned and marched off the flight deck.

"Whoa—who did that?" Rocket whispered, not knowing he echoed Ayesha's own question.

Peter Quill didn't have the time to speculate. "Don't know, doesn't matter," he replied urgently. "There's the jump point. Go! Go!"

The *Milano*'s engines opened up and powered

the battered ship as fast as they could toward the jump point that would send them to some semblance of haven.

"Hey, Quill!" Rocket called, still staring at the mysterious ship outside. "I think you're gonna want to come take a look at this."

There, standing on the edge of the oval-shaped ship, was the outline of a man. He seemed... relaxed yet powerful, as if the obliteration of an entire fleet was something he saw every day.

Quill caught a glimpse of the man as the *Milano* rapidly approached the jump point. He couldn't be entirely sure, but it seemed as though the man was staring right back at him, raising his hand in a casual wave just as the *Milano* disappeared into the space jump.

CHAPTER 7

"Okay, everybody," Peter Quill warned, "prepare yourselves for a really bad—"

He was cut off as the *Milano* smashed through a forest, flattening trees, splitting branches, and mowing through the underbrush. Looking around, he saw that everyone was safely strapped in, braced for impact—except for Groot, who was munching on candy as though it were popcorn and he was watching a movie.

"I am Groot!" he shouted in excitement, eyes wide open.

With a loud *thud*, the *Milano* broke through the thick foliage and landed on the cool surface of the planet Berhert, leaving a path of dirt and flattened brush behind it. Quill winced as he saw a mass of leaves and branches pressed against the window.

As everyone else tried to unbuckle their straps and get their bearings, Drax remained seated, breathing excitedly, as if he'd just been on a roller-coaster adventure. "That was amazing," he said, smiling.

Gamora rolled her eyes at him before turning her glare toward Rocket and Quill. "We could have died. Because of *your* arrogance," she yelled, exasperated.

Peter raised his hands defensively and turned

toward Rocket. "More like because *he* stole the Anulax batteries," he protested.

"You know why I did it, Star-Munch?" Rocket shot back. Quill crossed his arms, ignoring him. "Do you?" Rocket asked again.

"I'm not going to answer to 'Star-Munch,'" Peter retorted.

Rocket got in Quill's face. "I did it because I wanted to," he hissed. "And we would have escaped just fine if you could fly more like me and less like the Ravagers you grew up with."

"Jerk," Peter muttered.

"Thankfully, that tiny man on the ship saved us by blowing up an entire army with a blast of light," Rocket said, settling back in his chair.

"How tiny?" Drax asked.

Rocket demonstrated with his thumb and forefinger. "Like this."

"A one-inch-tall man saved us?" Gamora snorted.

"Well, if he got closer, I'm sure he'd be bigger," Rocket continued.

"That's how sight works, you silly raccoon!" Quill yelled, losing his patience with Rocket.

"Don't call me a raccoon!" Rocket yelled back.

"Oh, I'm sorry," Peter said in an overly exaggerated apologetic voice, "I meant to say 'trash panda'!"

Rocket opened his mouth to respond, but Quill's insult seemed to have caught him off-guard. Turning to Drax, he asked, "Is that better or worse?"

"I don't know," Drax replied with a shrug.

Quill turned to Drax, laughing. "It's worse."

Now Rocket was ready to respond. "You smelly, hairless—" he started to shout while lunging at Quill, when Groot suddenly jumped between the two, pointing up.

"I am Groot! I am Groot!" he repeated agitatedly.

Both Quill and Rocket stopped and looked in

disbelief in the direction Groot was pointing. The Guardians quickly ran to the back of the ship, now torn completely open, where Nebula was casually pointing up to the sky. "Someone followed you through the jump point," she said drily.

As the dust began to swirl around them, the Guardians drew their weapons, everyone standing back-to-back, ready to attack—or defend. Nebula tried to join them, but she was still chained to the *Milano*.

"Set me free," Nebula hissed at her sister. "You'll need my help."

Gamora scoffed at the suggestion. "I'm not a fool, Nebula," she responded.

Nebula shook her bonds at Gamora. "You're a fool if you leave one of your best hand-to-hand combatants chained up during a fight."

"You'll attack me the moment I let you go," Gamora countered.

"No, I won't," Nebula insisted—rather unconvincingly.

Quill, standing next to the bickering sisters, chimed in. "You'd think an evil supervillain would learn how to lie better." Just then, the ship Nebula pointed out—the same oval-shaped ship that had helped them escape the Sovereign fleet—landed, crushing all the trees around it.

Drax's eyes lit up. "I bet it's the one-inch man!" he said hopefully.

With a *hisssss* as the ship's cabin decompressed and a jet of steam came pouring out, a hatch opened. The outline of a man could be seen striding down. Although he had no recollection of ever seeing something or someone like this, Quill felt his stomach knot up. Something about this stranger felt familiar, like some kind of distant, faded memory. But why? All he could do was wait and find out.

Behind the mysterious man was a strange—but beautiful—woman with antennae. She looked at everyone in the group, one by one. The man's eyes, however, never left Peter. He burst into a charming smile.

"After all these years," he said, extending his arms toward Quill, "I've found you. I never thought I'd see you again, Peter."

Quill stood stiffly, still ready to use his weapons if it came to that. "Thanks for the assist back there," he said, his voice defiant, "but who are you? And how do you know my name?"

The man's roguish smile grew even larger as he strode closer, a familiar swagger to his walk. "I figured my rugged good looks would make it obvious to you, even after thirty years. My name's Ego," he continued, "and I'm your dad, Peter."

Peter Quill's weapon and jaw dropped at the same time.

CHAPTER 8

Despite its two huge overlapping suns, the planet Contraxia was as bitterly cold as the souls who dared visit its most infamous bar, the Iron Lotus. Located in a frenzied town of flashy buildings and neon lights, the Iron Lotus served a clientele primarily made up of Ravagers.

The Ravagers were sort of like an underground brotherhood—some might call them space pirates—dedicated to finding (or stealing, if necessary) objects of value throughout the galaxy and delivering them to the highest bidder. These objects weren't always considered "legal," but for Yondu Udonta, a job was a job. But even the Ravagers abided by certain unspoken codes, and Yondu's "a job is a job" approach sometimes crossed the line. His reputation was growing among the Ravagers, and not in a good way.

Yondu quietly exited his suite at the Iron Lotus and glanced over at an older Ravager, Tullk, who nodded back to him. Two bodyguards immediately flanked them. Together, they entered the main barroom of the Iron Lotus, where the sound of a familiar voice stopped Yondu in his tracks.

Swearing under his breath, Yondu scanned the room. A group of Ravagers in blue uniforms was seated around a table. The voice Yondu had recognized came from a huge man—a legend among the Ravagers. It was best to be either on his good side or not on his radar at all. Unfortunately, Yondu was neither.

The Ravager was in the middle of a boisterous tale. "And I was like, 'Aleta, I love you, but you're crazy; you always been crazy—'"

Just then, he spotted Yondu. Yondu had no choice. He decided the best course of action was to face his fellow Ravagers like a man. A terrified man, but a man nonetheless.

"Been some time," Yondu said with as much confidence as he could muster. The blue-skinned Ravager fell into a seat.

"Seems like this establishment is the wrong kind of disreputable," the huge man growled. There was venom in his voice.

The grizzled Ravager ignored Yondu and instead spoke in the direction of the Iron Lotus's owner, a Sneeper. "There are a hundred Ravager factions," he called. "You just lost the business of ninety-nine by serving one."

"Please, sir," the owner begged from behind the counter. "Please!"

Yondu watched as the rest of his gang, along with everyone else in the room, emptied the saloon. In short order, the only people left were Yondu and the rest of his crew, including a man named Kraglin, Yondu's right hand. They all looked expectantly to Yondu. Yondu jumped up from the seat, his jaw set in grim determination, and marched outside.

In the freezing wind and snow, Yondu called out. "You know what? I don't care what you think of me!"

"Then why you following us for?" the true leader of the Ravagers asked, turning to face Yondu, fists clenched.

"'Cause you'll listen to what I gotta say," Yondu

spat back, his own arms braced in a defensive posture, in case it came to that.

"I don't got to listen to nothing!" the big man scoffed. "You betrayed the code. Ravagers don't deal in—"

"I didn't know what the cargo was!" Yondu interrupted. "All I knew is someone was paying a pretty penny for it!"

"Don't lie to my face, Yondu." He sneered. He leaned in toward Yondu, who flinched slightly. "You didn't know 'cause you chose not to know, 'cause it made you rich!"

The Ravager turned to walk away, but his point was clearly lost on Yondu, who yelled, "I demand a seat at the table! I wear the flames, same as you!"

The battle-worn Ravager had seen others banished—but he, himself, had never done it. For a Ravager, it was a punishment almost worse than death. But he knew it must be done. Squaring his shoulders again, he turned back to face Yondu.

"Yondu Udonta," he began, "you may dress like a Ravager, but you won't hear no Horns of Freedom when you die, and the colors of Ogord will *not* flash over your grave. You think I take some pleasure in exiling you? You're wrong. You broke all our hearts. May our paths never cross again."

With that, the Ravagers stormed off into the snowy night.

Standing alone outside the Iron Lotus, Yondu felt the snow fall gently on his skin as the only way of life he'd ever known was ripped away from him.

Well behind him, Yondu's crew huddled closer together. They saw their leader stripped of his status, and they wondered what that might mean for them. Either way, the murmurs of mutiny began to spread among the group.

"First, Quill betrays us and Yondu just lets

him go scot-free," whispered a monstrously large Ravager named Taserface. "Now he's gettin' all riled over nothing. We followed him 'cause he was the one who wasn't afraid to do what needed to be done." He gestured at the crushed-looking Yondu, standing alone in the snow. "Seems like he's going soft."

"If he's so soft, why you whispering for?" challenged Kraglin.

Taserface stared Kraglin dead in the eyes. Without blinking, he said, "You know I'm right, Kraglin."

Tullk stepped between the two men and warned, "You'd best watch what you say about the capt'n, Ta—"

A sleek vessel landing in front of the Iron Lotus stopped him mid-sentence. As the doors opened, two Sovereign chambermaids rolled out a long blue cloth that stopped exactly at Yondu's feet. High Priestess Ayesha passed by the crew of Ravagers, ignoring them. Stopping at the end of the blue cloth, she forced a smile. So soft was her walk that Yondu hadn't heard her.

"Yondu Udonta," she said, her voice startling him as he turned to face her. "I have a proposition for you."

As white snow fell on his blue skin, Yondu considered his options. Seeing as he was no longer a Ravager, he didn't have many left. With his signature smirk, he cocked his head slightly, all ears.

CHAPTER 9

Ever since Peter Quill had learned he was only half human, he had wondered what the other half was. Would he suddenly sprout wings one day? Turn blue and grow gills to swim underwater? The possibilities had seemed endless. Instead, looking at Ego eating heartily across the campfire, he realized his other half was just…this *man*. Apparently an incredibly powerful man who wiped out fleets of spaceships for fun—but still, just a man. Part of Peter was relieved, but mostly, after all these years, he was filled with questions.

"Why?" he asked bluntly.

Ego didn't need the question to be expanded. He knew where his son was coming from.

"Your mother was dying," he replied, "so I hired Yondu to pick you up."

"Maybe you should check babysitter references," Quill muttered under his breath.

"I would have come for you myself," Ego continued, "but I was in the midst of an intergalactic battle against demonic forces and trying to save this dimension. I think. They all start to bleed together." He tried to explain as best he could. "Yondu was supposed to return you, but he kept you for himself. I have no idea why."

Quill scoffed, recalling his younger days. "Because

I was a skinny kid who could squeeze into places adults couldn't," he said. "Easier for thieving."

"Believe me, my son, I've been trying to find you ever since," Ego entreated, true remorse in his eyes.

"I thought Yondu *was* your father?" Drax piped up, slightly confused.

"What?!" Quill was amazed at how dense his teammate could be sometimes.

"You look exactly alike," Drax muttered in his own defense.

Rocket rolled his eyes and laughed. "One's blue!" he said.

Even Groot looked at Drax in disbelief. "I am Groot," he said, shaking his head.

"Yondu wasn't a father," Quill said, speaking almost to himself. "He was the guy who abducted me, taught me how to fight, and kept me in constant terror by threatening to eat me!" He was getting completely worked up just from the memories.

"Eat you?!" Ego exclaimed in horror. His eyes narrowed. "That low-down, dirty—"

Gamora interrupted. "After all this time, how did you locate us now?" she asked, a slight suspicion in her voice.

Ego stood, proudly looking at his son. "Even where I reside," he began, "out past the edge of what is known, we've heard tell of the man they call Star-Lord."

Quill's chest puffed up with pride. "Ha! See? Told ya!" he said before noticing that no one was impressed. He turned his attention back to his father, who was still looking only at him.

"What do you say we head there now?" Ego asked.

"Past the edge of what is known?" Gamora asked, eyebrow raised.

Ego just continued to address Quill directly. "You

and the rest of your associates are welcome," he said, "even the triangle-faced monkey there. I promise you, it's like nothing you've ever seen before." Ego paused, then continued softly. "And there I can explain your very special heritage in much more detail. Everything will be made clear."

Quill stared at Ego. The father-son trip he'd longed for since he was a child was actually going to become a reality. The answers he'd longed for all his life were a hyper-jump away. So why wouldn't his mouth open and yell, "Of course! Let's go!"?

A light touch on his arm broke his daydream. It was Gamora. "Peter, we need to go for a walk," she said.

Ego stretched his arms, realizing his moment had been interrupted. "And I need to go to the bathroom," he quipped. "Everybody needs some-thing around here."

Whistling, Ego walked off into the bushes as Gamora and Peter headed in the other direction, behind the *Milano*. Groot, Rocket, and Drax remained by the campfire with the woman who had come off the spaceship with Ego. Her name was Mantis. After a few moments of silence, Drax looked at Mantis, who was staring back at him, her mouth stretched into a creepy, too-wide smile.

"What are you doing?" Drax asked, unnerved.

"Smiling," Mantis said, without changing her expression. "I have heard it is the thing to do to make people like you."

Drax shook his head and said, "Not if you do it like that."

Mantis dropped her exaggerated smile. "Oh." She sighed, slightly embarrassed. "I was raised alone on Ego's planet. I do not understand the complexities of social interaction."

"I am an excellent teacher. You may follow what I do and learn much," Drax offered helpfully.

Rocket was busy checking one of his weapons, paying no attention to Drax or Mantis. "Of course Quill's dad *would* be named 'Ego,'" he muttered. "All makes sense now."

Pointing at Rocket, Mantis gave a slight grin of excitement. "Can I pet your puppy?" she asked Drax. "It is adorable!"

Drax looked over at the unaware Rocket, a mischievous grin crossing his face. "Yes," he said. "He loves to be scratched behind the ears."

Mantis moved toward Rocket, reaching out to rub him behind his ears. Rocket spotted movement out of the corner of his eye and immediately turned and snapped, almost biting Mantis's hand.

Mantis pulled away her hand and scooted back to Drax, giggling. Drax was laughing heartily.

"That," he said, "is called a practical joke!"

She looked at Drax, joy in her eyes. "I liked it very much!" she exclaimed.

Drax smiled at Mantis in appreciation. He could get along well with her.

In a clearing behind the *Milano*, Gamora found herself trying to convince Quill of the dangers of following the man claiming to be his father into the unknown reaches of the galaxy, but his mind seemed made up.

"We have no reason to believe he's actually your father," Gamora said as patiently as possible. "This feels like an easy trap. Kree purists, the Ravagers, now the Sovereign—who could have easily tracked us. They all want us dead."

Peter pointed in the direction of Ego. "Not him," he said. "He saved our lives."

Gamora sighed in exasperation but continued. "We saved Nebula's—for the bounty. Who says he isn't doing the same? Or for any other reason we can't see yet?"

"Look," Quill said, holding a worn photo, "when I was a kid, I'd carry around this picture of this guy I told people was my dad."

Gamora stared at it blankly. "Who is that?"

"A super-cool guy who was a singer and an actor on a show where his car talked," Quill explained.

"Why did it talk?" Gamora asked, confused.

"To fight crime and be a good pal," he said, shrugging.

Gamora didn't understand what a talking car had to do with anything, but she sensed Quill was opening up to her. "That's really sweet, Peter," she said, reaching out to touch Quill's hand before he pulled it away, "but—"

"No, it's sad," he countered. "Everyone knew that wasn't my real dad. I'd see all the other kids with their dads.... All I wanted more than anything was to have my own father. What if this is my chance?" Quill's voice broke slightly.

"Who says we shouldn't check out who he *really* is?" Quill continued, his eyes full of longing. Gamora knew there was no talking him out of this. She gave a very slight nod, then turned and walked back toward the campfire. Quill did a tiny fist pump behind her. His dream was coming true. Or so he hoped.

Moments later, inside the *Milano*, Gamora was packing up their gear while her sister screamed,

"You're leaving me with that fox?!" Nebula was incensed.

Rocket threw down a wrench, reached for a blaster, and said, "How many times do I have to say it? *Not. A. Fox!*"

"Shoot her if she does anything suspicious," Gamora instructed, glancing at Nebula. "Or if you feel like it. Just keep her alive." Rocket grunted in disappointment at that last part.

A small voice spoke up from behind Gamora. "I am Groot." He looked as if he was about to cry.

Gamora picked him up gently. "It will just be a couple days," she explained. "We'll be back before Rocket's finished fixing the ship."

She set him back down, and he went over to Rocket, ready to cry on his shoulder. "Watch it— you know I hate getting wet," Rocket said in his own consoling way. "We've been alone before, pal. This is nothing."

The group gathered outside Ego's ship, where he was waiting to welcome them. "I'm glad you've decided to take this trip," he said to Quill. "Hopefully it's the first step in making things up to you." Ego patted his son's shoulder and entered the ship with Mantis.

Drax, Gamora, and Quill looked back at the Guardians they were leaving behind. "Don't break my ship any more than it is, fuzzy!" Quill called out to Rocket.

"Hope your daddy isn't as big of a jerk as you, orphan boy," Rocket shot back.

Quill smiled. Drax and Gamora entered the ship, but he hesitated and took one last look at the *Milano*. Groot was waving good-bye wildly. Quill felt that familiar sense of nerves and adrenaline rise in his chest as he turned to enter Ego's ship. His first father-son adventure, his childhood dream, was about to begin.

He is a fantastic pilot and flies his ship, the *Milano*, through all sorts of mayhem.

Even if he tends to get himself in trouble—at his core, Peter is a pretty great guy.

Peter Quill was born on Terra, aka Earth, but was abducted when he was small. He's spent his life traveling the galaxy and trying to earn a reputation as the legendary outlaw Star-Lord.

The Guardians of the Galaxy think so, too. Gamora and Drax are excellent fighters and incredibly dangerous— but are also loyal friends. With Rocket and Groot filling out the roster, the Guardians are a formidable team.

Their adventures are dangerous, and the stakes are high, but the Guardians are a family of sorts.

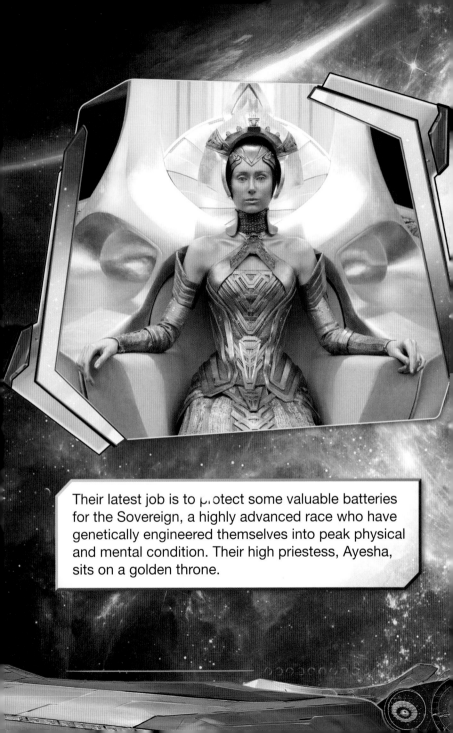

Their latest job is to protect some valuable batteries for the Sovereign, a highly advanced race who have genetically engineered themselves into peak physical and mental condition. Their high priestess, Ayesha, sits on a golden throne.

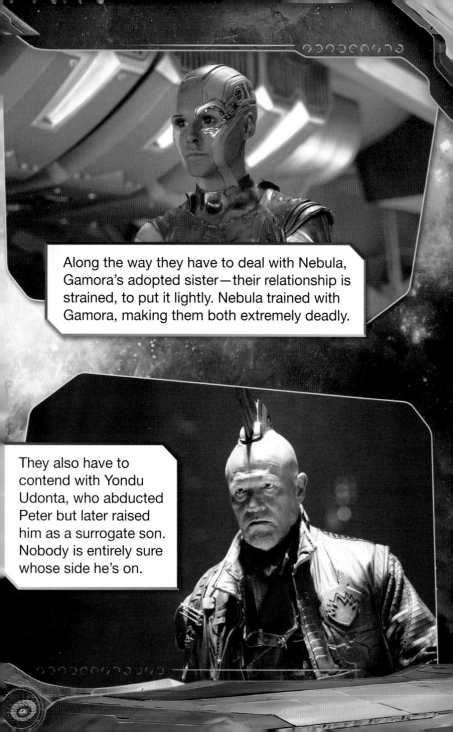

Along the way they have to deal with Nebula, Gamora's adopted sister—their relationship is strained, to put it lightly. Nebula trained with Gamora, making them both extremely deadly.

They also have to contend with Yondu Udonta, who abducted Peter but later raised him as a surrogate son. Nobody is entirely sure whose side he's on.

Yondu is the leader of a group of thieves and mercenaries called the Ravagers…

…but lately his leadership has been called into question. The Ravagers were heroes in the battle for Xandar, but they might not have noble intentions anymore.

Through all of this, there's a mysterious man called Ego, who claims to be Peter's actual father. Peter is unsure what that means for him.

Along with his equally mysterious companion, Mantis, Ego sets out to prove his trustworthiness to the Guardians.

The Guardians of the Galaxy must stick together and fight whatever threat comes next…

…even if it involves a really big and delicate bomb.

CHAPTER 10

The firelight crackled as all four moons of Berhert hit their zenith, casting a light-blue glow. Inside the *Milano*, Rocket hummed along to a catchy tune from Quill's Awesome Mix Tape Vol. 2, absent-mindedly chewing on a cut piece of wire as he examined the damage caused by the fight with the Sovereign fleet and the crash landing (none of which was his fault, of course).

"Hey, you—fox. Do you have any actual food lying around this garbage heap?" Nebula asked grumpily.

"I'm not talking to you until you stop calling me names," Rocket shot back.

"What name did I call you?" Nebula asked, genuinely confused and increasingly annoyed.

"I am Groot," said a small voice, the little Guardian shaking a branch at her as though she should know better.

"Exactly," Rocket agreed, nodding and going back to work.

"Exactly what? I don't speak tiny-tree language," Nebula snarled.

"Well, talking to my friend with that attitude isn't going to do you any favors." Rocket gave Groot a high five.

Nebula rattled her chains, fed up with the two. "Can't you go forage for some food in the forest?"

she demanded. "How are you the one in charge of fixing the spaceship, anyway? No wonder it looks like a child built it!"

"Just for that, no foraged food for Miss Cranky Pants. Got it, Groot?" Rocket responded.

Groot smiled. "I am Groot," he said with a salute.

"Oh, but can ya be a pal and bring me a bit of that Xandarian-cured meat I know Drax keeps hidden under his bunk?" Rocket asked, winking at Nebula. "All this hard work—I'm starving!"

"I'll roast you over this fire like the rodent you are," Nebula growled.

"*Ooooooh*, I'm shaking in my boots," Rocket whimpered. Then he became more serious and approached Nebula. "Look, we're both thieves, right? Theoretically, we *should* like each other or have a little honor. Problem is, every time I've seen you, you wanna kill me or one of my friends. Too bad, 'cause I can be a pretty good pal. But try and

come for me, even out here? I'll always get the first shot." Rocket was menacingly close to Nebula now. Suddenly his face dropped back into a smile as Groot tossed him the meat. "Time to feast like a king! Glad we came to this understanding. I feel the air is cleared—do you feel the air is clearer, pal?"

"I am Groot," his companion said matter-of-factly.

Nebula gave him a sinister glare, clearly plotting the different ways she'd hurt Rocket as soon as she was free. She slumped back against the ship and looked into the sky as Rocket started humming again, now adding a little dance to his step.

Deep in the woods towering over the *Milano*, menacing eyes peered down on the unaware

Rocket. Taserface, the monstrous Ravager, and Kraglin, Yondu's right hand, quietly crested a hilltop to get a better view of the grounded ship and its occupants.

"Finally," Taserface growled. "Our chance to get some real vengeance on Quill and his gnats."

"I'm sure Yondu—" Kraglin began, before being interrupted by a sneer from the huge Ravager.

"'Sure Yondu' what, Kraglin? 'Cause I think he's just playing lapdog to that gold lady. He may be the hired gun, but only someone with power like hers could get us *this*." Taserface swept his arm behind him. Descending into the valley were dozens of M-ships landing softly on the other side of the ridge from the *Milano*. Within moments, there were squads of Ravagers pouring out from each ship, all moving to the top of the hill. Standing in the center, like a king who'd finally reclaimed his throne, was Yondu. Aware of all the eyes on him,

he took a moment to savor the sweet turn fortune had given him.

Yondu looked over at Kraglin a few yards away and nodded at his trusted ally. Turning back to the troops, he waved his hand for them to follow, swiftly but quietly.

"Don't forget it was Yondu she hired, not you, Taserface," Kraglin warned. Taserface scoffed and marched along with the rest of the Ravagers.

As the Ravagers began to circle the *Milano*, Taserface's adrenaline rose. He was ready to attack! He could hear Rocket humming a soft, upbeat dance hit as he moved around in the small arc cast by the lights of the *Milano*. He couldn't wait any longer. He glanced at the Ravager next to him, who looked wild-eyed and completely unhinged, and gave a big thumbs-up. Then they both crashed through the brush and began to run toward the *Milano*. But Taserface couldn't keep up. Nor could he warn his

fellow Ravager when he heard a *click* as he stomped right onto a trap buried in the underbrush.

Taserface quickly hit the ground and yelled, "Trap!" His warning was too late, however, as almost a hundred darts suddenly shot directly at the Ravagers from the treetops. As the darts hit their marks, the Ravagers fell by the dozens. The Ravager who'd set off the trap was still standing there, looking around in amazement and confusion. Before he could take another step, though, a dart hit him, and he fell to the ground.

Deep inside the *Milano*, the sound of the shot woke Nebula with a jolt. She could still hear Rocket humming, but in an odd, repetitive way. Just then, she noticed he had taped a walkie-talkie to the open window and pointed it outward so the speakers faced the woods. "Idiot *wants* us to get killed," Nebula muttered, shaking her head and looking at Groot, who was cowering in the corner.

"I am Groot," he said, genuinely afraid Rocket may have gotten them in over their heads this time.

Rocket slung his rifle over his shoulder and pulled out a remote detonator with two buttons on it. One was labeled BANG, the other, BIGGER BANG. Crouched in a tree above the *Milano* and still humming his song into his comm, Rocket extended the antenna of the detonator and watched as two Ravager squadrons drew closer and closer. With a gleam in his eye, Rocket pressed the bang button. One entire squadron flew into the air as an electro-current blast shot through them. The other squadron stopped in its tracks. *Perfect place*, Rocket thought with a grin. The bigger-bang button lived up to its name as the squadron—and part of a nearby tree—suffered the same electro-current blast as its accomplices.

Rocket's giggles interrupted his humming on the radio, and one of the Ravagers spotted him. "There!" shouted the Ravager, but it was too late. Rocket propelled himself from one tree branch to another and began pushing buttons in alternate sequences, making Ravager after Ravager fly up into the air until the electro-current concussive blasts ran out of energy.

Back on the *Milano*, Nebula tried her best to plead with Groot, but it wasn't working. "Your friend, the furry one, he's in serious danger," she said. "He needs my help." She held out her shackles. "Please, let me go join him."

Groot looked at her suspiciously. "I am Groot?"

Nebula sighed. "If you're talking about when I said I'd fry him, I take it back, okay?" she bargained sweetly, but Groot did not look convinced. The sound of Rocket leaping and grunting as he moved from branch to branch gave Nebula

an idea. "Look, Groot, just hand me that comm unit. I think I have an idea."

Groot was used to hearing his fellow Guardians say those words, and they almost always ended up leaving them in worse situations. *But what's the worst she could do with a communication unit?* he figured.

Several yards outside, Rocket crouched quietly in a tree as a half dozen Ravagers made their way through the forest looking for him. Rocket held his breath and waited—and waited—until the last one passed. Smiling, Rocket dropped down onto the shoulder of the last man in the squadron and took out a handful of small, sticky discs. He slapped one onto the man's back and then leaped forward, slapping another onto the shoulder blades of the man

directly in front of him, and then leaped again, and so on until he reached the front of the squadron. All the Ravagers were wildly flailing about trying to reach for the discs, but they couldn't grasp them.

"Here ya go, fellas. Lemme get those for ya," Rocket said as he pulled out a small device with a switch. Jumping high into the air, he flipped the switch, and the Ravagers all began to twitch as electricity flowed through the discs. They flopped around and then fell all at once.

Rocket was so busy laughing, he didn't notice a bulky Ravager named Brahl and his tough compatriot approaching from opposite sides.

"Ain't so tough now without your little toys, are ya?" Brahl taunted.

"Who needs toys when I can just borrow yours?" Rocket asked. "I'll just kick you in the face and have your friend shoot you. Wanna see? It's pretty cool." Rocket crouched low as he spoke.

Without warning, Rocket leaped into the air, punching Brahl. The second Ravager fired, but Rocket backflipped out of the way, and the blast hit Brahl instead. Rocket landed on the second Ravager's head and rapid-punched until both Ravagers were lying unconscious, Rocket standing between them.

"See? I told ya. No toys, and I still—" Rocket gloated before being cut off by the eerily familiar sound of a high-pitched whistle slicing through the night air. He looked up just in time to see Yondu's arrow streaking down, straight toward him.

Rocket braced himself. But another whistle caused the arrow to stop suddenly, suspended just in front of Rocket's forehead.

"Hey there, rat," came the gravelly voice of Yondu Udonta as he walked out of the forest, a large smile on his face. "Aren't you glad to see me?"

CHAPTER 11

Nebula signaled to a trembling Groot to stay quiet as the unlikely duo huddled in their hiding place within the *Milano*. They watched as the Ravagers, led by Yondu, marched Rocket toward the ship, an arrow floating dangerously close to the Guardian's head.

"Any minute, baby tree," she whispered. "I hope," she added under her breath to herself.

As Rocket was being led to the *Milano*, he tried to engage his captors in conversation while he thought of his next move. "So, Yondu, how's life been, ya big blue idiot?" he asked as casually as possible.

"Not so bad." Yondu chuckled, now that he had Rocket trapped and was on his way to accomplishing his mission. "We got a pretty good gig. A golden gal with quite a high opinion of herself."

"You two must get along great." Rocket sneered, thinking back to his last interaction with High Priestess Ayesha.

"Ha." Yondu laughed. "Too uptight for me, but the money she offered up for you and your pals will do just fine. Sounds like you got on the wrong side of her radar. As usual. Luckily, she was able to show me your last known location. The jump point was pretty easy to figure out after that—I just looked

for the most hospitable planet nearby, knowing how much you mucked up your ship here." Yondu nodded to the damaged *Milano*.

Kraglin leaned in to Yondu and asked, "What about the tracer we put on the hull during the war over Xandar?"

"That was a backup," Yondu growled. "I got us here, didn't I?"

"Yes, boss," Kraglin said, nodding meekly.

"And I captured the rodent, didn't I?" Yondu asked, louder this time, addressing the larger group.

A halfhearted chorus of *yeahs; sure thing, Capt'ns;* and *uh-huh*s came from the dozen or so remaining Ravagers.

"So this gold chick...she's paying you to kill us?" Rocket asked, a plan forming in his head.

"Plus a bonus if we return the stolen batteries," Yondu answered.

Rocket turned quickly to face his captors. "You

give your word you won't hurt Groot an' me, and I'll tell you where the batteries are," he said.

Yondu grinned, his craggy teeth shining. "Lucky for you my word don't mean squat. If it did, I'd actually hand you over to that lady. Money talks, furball."

Taserface stood erect to his monstrous height. "You're just gonna let them go?" he demanded. "That woman offered us a million for the batteries *plus* whatever we can get for their—"

"Who's the captain around here?" Yondu responded, his voice steady with authority. "Besides, we can get more for the batteries individually than what she's offerin'."

As Yondu spoke, Rocket noticed something in the forest behind the Ravagers, a movement so subtle that the branches barely shook. Suddenly, he was filled with hope. All he had to do was keep the Ravagers distracted.

"I'm with Yondu on this one," Rocket chimed

in. "All you need is any fried furry thing and..." He spun around, fell on the ground, stuck out his tongue, and played dead.

"Get up, you idiot," Yondu said, prodding him with his boot.

Without moving, his eyes squinted shut, Rocket muttered out of the corner of his mouth, "Can't... move.... I'm dead...."

Yondu sighed and said, "Look, we're on a timetable, and it doesn't include your little theater in the park. So be a good pet and get me those batteries, and we'll be on our way."

Taserface reached for his weapon and snarled. "I think you've gone a little soft, Yondu—maybe it's time for new leadership."

Yondu's blue face flushed as he saw the mutiny unfolding before him. "We're not stupid enough to actually kill the Guardians of the Galaxy!" he fumed. "We'd have the whole Nova Corps on us."

Another tough-looking Ravager drew his weapon as well. "Maybe with the right one in charge, we could handle them," he said.

Sensing the support growing for him, the monstrous Taserface widened his mouth into a terrifying grin, showing two rows of teeth. "I don't give a spit about the Nova Corps," he snarled, "but you sure seem to be worried about a lot of things these days. Not focused on doin' yer job as a leader." Turning his back on Yondu, he addressed the other Ravagers, his voice booming: "Who's with me?"

A chorus of *aye*s roared through the forest.

Yondu seethed in anger at this sudden betrayal. "You wouldn't dare." He sneered. "None of ya know the ways this galaxy operates. None of ya are fit ta lead!" Turning to the only person he thought he could trust, Yondu felt almost desperate. "Tell 'em I'm right, Kraglin," he said.

Kraglin could only kick the dirt, his eyes not

meeting his leader's. "I—I'm not sure, Yondu," he said haltingly. "Maybe it's best we let someone new try. Just for a little bit."

"Someone *new*?!" Yondu roared. "Like who?"

"I nominate me," Taserface growled.

In a flash, the large Ravager had Yondu's hands cuffed in chains. He was so close Yondu could smell the rations Taserface had been eating earlier.

The other Ravagers began to chant, "Taserface! Captain! Taserface!" He stood to his full height, looking down at Yondu.

"Now salute," the mutineer bellowed, prompting a chorus of derisive laughter among the Ravagers. Yondu didn't move. Never in his decades of travels with the Ravagers did he imagine he'd face such a mutiny.

At his feet, Yondu heard a sharp whisper. "Hey, Boy Blue." It was Rocket. "Maybe it's a good idea ta do what he says. Like, right about now."

Yondu looked fiercely at Rocket. "You with them, too?" he hissed.

Rocket shrugged. "Your death," he said. "But don't say I never tried to help you out." Yondu simply glared at him in response.

Rocket looked nervously at the trees. No movement. Turning his attention back to the mounting tension, he waved his hands in the air. "Hold on!" he shouted up at Taserface. The other Ravagers all hushed and stared at him. "There's got to be some sort of peaceful resolution here! Or even a violent resolution . . . where I'm standing over *there*!"

Suddenly, as if on cue, two blasts rang out. Rocket looked down at his body—he was still in one piece. The blasts had knocked the guns from the Ravagers' hands. Everyone looked around. A voice came from the tree line.

"*Not* killing the Guardians is the smartest thing I think I've ever heard you say, Yondu." At that

moment, a light began to radiate, illuminating the tree line. It revealed the white ship belonging to Ego. Star-Lord, blasters drawn, was standing on top of it. The hatch opened, and Gamora and Drax rushed out, ready for battle.

A handful of Ravagers turned toward the Guardians and rushed to attack, Taserface leading the way. Drax and Gamora met them head-on. They whirled in a blur as they quickly disarmed the Ravagers. Drax took particular pleasure in knocking Taserface out cold. But Rocket couldn't let them have all the fun. He sprang onto a Ravager's back, scrambling up and down the Ravager, biting his ears and punching him until he eventually fell to the ground.

"*That's* for not staying down earlier!" Rocket said, wiping his hands clean on his uniform.

Smiling nervously, Yondu stepped forward. "Quill, my boy," he said. "Good to see you. Your

little friend and I were just closing a deal to make sure—"

Star-Lord backed away from the blue-skinned Ravager. "Not so fast," he said. "There's someone here who'd probably like to say a thing or two to you. Remember how you were supposed to raise me all safe and sound? Yeah, about that…"

"We had a deal, Yondu," came a voice from inside the ship. Yondu paled at the sound of it, knowing the speaker before Ego emerged, eyes narrowed.

"N-never thought I'd see you again," Yondu stuttered.

"No, you were too busy recruiting my son into a life of thievery and debauchery," Ego said. "But it is all in the past. What's done is done." Ego glanced at his son and continued. "We have bigger things to take care of," he said, without giving any further details.

"Well, if ya don't mind, looks like you folks have

some catching up to do, so why don't we just part ways here?" Yondu said.

Ego shrugged and turned to leave, but Quill nudged him. "Can we at least do something about that?" he asked, pointing to the handcuffs on Yondu's wrists. "I mean, he's not perfect, but he did raise me like his own son."

Ego's eyes flicked over Yondu, then took in the crowd of mutinous Ravagers standing farther back. "I do believe we have one more bit of business," he said.

A small beam of light streamed from Ego's fingertip. Yondu closed his eyes and braced himself. Then, he heard a *clink* at his feet. Looking down, he saw the cuffs that had bound him had fallen off. Ego knew Yondu could have done a lot worse raising Peter, and in his own way, he was grateful that Peter grew up with someone to look up to—even if Yondu did threaten occasionally to eat him.

The other Ravagers huddled nervously. "What are you gonna do to us?" Kraglin asked, his voice shaking.

"You will not be taking any prisoners back to the Sovereign," Ego said to Kraglin. "You will follow the orders of your *rightful* captain, Yondu."

"Y-yes, yes, sir," Kraglin stuttered.

"That's right," Yondu shouted, his confidence rising again now that the mutiny had been quelled. He walked to where Taserface still lay unconscious and firmly placed the cuffs that once held him on the mutineer's arms. "And we got a lotta talking to do," he growled.

"Remember, stay away from Ayesha and the rest of the Sovereign," Quill warned. "As far as they know, you never found us!"

Yondu gave Quill a thumbs-up and winked at him. "You got it, my boy!" he replied with a wave.

The Ravagers hurried away, boarded their ships, and took off. Rocket watched them go and let out a big sigh of relief. "Well, *that* went exceedingly not the way I had planned. Not that I mind the assist, Quill, but how in the world did you know to—"

Gamora held up a walkie. Rocket, looking confused, said, "But I wasn't on your channel."

"Ahem," came a voice from behind. Rocket turned to see Nebula holding another walkie-talkie, Groot standing beside her.

"I am Groot!" said Groot with a grin.

"Your tiny tree wouldn't unshackle me to help fight," Nebula explained, "so I took a chance that your friends might still be in range." She paused and waited for some sort of thanks.

Rocket gave Groot a wink and said, "Great thinking, pal!"

Nebula sighed and tossed the walkie-talkie away.

"My sister's gambit paid off. For that, I suppose some gratitude is in order," Gamora said reluctantly. "You're still being turned in for ransom when we return."

"I feel so loved." Nebula sneered and walked back into the *Milano*.

Quill clapped his hands together to get everyone's attention. "Okay, warm and fuzzies all taken care of? Great. As far as the Sovereign know, we're lost, and the Ravagers are... well, as competent as Ravagers can be." He rolled his eyes before continuing. "But for now, I think we should stick together as a team, in case we encounter any more little surprises. Rocket and Groot, you're coming with us. My dad wants to fly us off on some secret mission at the edge of the universe—which sounds totally awesome."

Groot jumped up and boarded Ego's ship, cheering, "I am Groot!" Gamora and Drax checked

Nebula's shackles, then turned to follow Groot onto the ship. Quill was about to join them, but Rocket held him back for a moment. "Hey, uh, Quill, thanks for coming back and not screwing up saving us," he said. "You're full of surprises, I guess."

Quill turned to look at his teammate. "Those two sisters may hate each other, but we're the Guardians of the Galaxy, man. We gotta look out for each other," he said, smiling. "Nobody else is."

With that, the two Guardians entered Ego's ship, the hatch closed, and they took off, once again leaving for parts unknown. Watching the forest disappear below them, Rocket knew that even if the Guardians had no idea where they were going next, his friends would have his back anywhere in the galaxy.

BONUS

**INCLUDES AN EXCLUSIVE
GUARDIANS STORY YOU
WON'T SEE IN THEATERS!**

Hey, Quill!" came a voice over a comm unit. "Your ship's the worst!"

Peter Quill gasped for a breath of air that was barely there. He didn't appreciate anyone taking a jab at his beloved *Milano*. And he especially didn't appreciate anyone taking a jab at his beloved *Milano* while he was desperately trying to fix her.

"We can talk about my ship later. And shut up," Quill said, annoyed. "I can hardly breathe! If we don't find some way of plugging this hull breach, we're gonna lose all oxygen and cabin pressure in just a few—"

"If you can hardly breathe, then why are you still talking?" asked Rocket, with obvious snark. "Shouldn't you be trying to conserve oxygen, like the rest of us?"

Quill rolled his eyes, and gasped for another breath of oxygen. "Look who's talking! And I mean *talking*! Talkity-talk-talk-talk…"

"Whatever," Rocket replied. "You want to do this? Fine, let's do it!" he said, shifting in the pilot's seat.

"I am Groot," said a treelike being who was definitely more sapling than full-grown tree.

"Right, you're right," Rocket said, nodding at Groot. Some time had passed since Groot had sacrificed himself to save his teammates. The twig that Rocket had recovered from his friend was growing fast. "We'll settle this later." Rocket struggled with the *Milano*'s controls, a ship that was sluggish at best, unresponsive at worst.

And that was when Quill was sucked out into space.

* * *

Peter was annoyed, but this wasn't anything new. Rocket could be hot-tempered and say lots of things he shouldn't, but he was great in a fight. *He also thinks he's a pilot*, Peter thought, *which is a laugh because I am the pilot.*

Pause.

I am the pilot who's floating outside of his own disabled ship, drifting off into space with less than a minute of oxygen left in his mask.

As Peter floated, he inspected his ship. Something had struck its hull at high speed, disabling most of the ship's systems. The *Milano* began to lose oxygen at a startling rate, prompting Peter and his teammates to attempt an emergency patch on the hull breach. As the oxygen levels sank and the cabin pressure fluctuated wildly, it was only a matter of time before someone was sucked through the breach and out into the void of space.

Now, with only a minute of reserve oxygen in his Star-Lord mask, the clock was ticking. *I hate when Rocket's right*, he thought.

* * *

"Drax!" Rocket gasped. "Aren't you listening? Quill's floating away, he needs—"

Rocket turned his head away from the *Milano*'s controls, and toward Drax, who wasn't there. Then he let out an exasperated sigh. "I needed that guy to do one thing—one thing! And now Quill is gonna drift off into space forever and ever. Can we fire him? Do we really want a guy like that around?"

Rocket prepared for another outburst, when something caught his eye outside the cockpit. He saw Quill, adrift. And that's when he saw Drax. The tattooed warrior, attached to the ship via tether, grabbed Peter.

"You're not gonna tell him I said all that stuff, right?" Rocket said to the green-skinned woman standing right next to him.

"We have a problem," she said.

"What problem, Gamora?" Rocket rejoined. "The ship doesn't work, Quill almost died trying to fix it, Drax doesn't listen to anyone and just does what he wants, and you're telling me there's a *problem*?"

Gamora said nothing in response. She let her icy stare and demeanor do the talking.

"I am Groot," chimed in Groot.

Rocket sighed again, this time louder. "Fine, she's right, so what?" he said. "You're a buzzkill, pal."

* * *

Peter Quill was back safely aboard the *Milano*. An emergency patch was in place. Mostly. The Guardians of the Galaxy had regrouped, assessed their predicament, and agreed the situation looked far less grim than it had before.

The situation still looked grim. Really grim.

"What's the problem again?" asked Peter, scratching the back of his head.

Gamora stared at the man some called Star-Lord. Her emotions were impossible to read. "Do I need to explain it again, Peter?" she said.

"Yes," said Drax. "You should explain it over and over again for our benefit."

Peter broke out in a smile. "No, no, I'm just having fun. I'm not sure about Drax; he might be having fun, too? Hard to tell. But I get it; I get the problem. It's a big problem," he said playfully.

Rocket looked at Groot, and shook his head. "This guy does understand that our ship is dead in space, right? The controls are shot. And we still have a big hole to worry about. That patch ain't gonna hold for long."

"I am Groot," said Groot.

"Exactly," Rocket agreed. It was true. Over the course of the past hour, the ship went from functional to mostly functional to somewhat functional to hot, immobile mess. They still had no idea as to what struck their vessel.

"We sit here doing nothing," Gamora stated flatly, turning to face Peter. "We are alone and vulnerable in space, and all you can do is make jokes?"

Gamora was an imposing figure, and anyone else might have backed down. But Peter Quill was not anyone else. The half-human son of an Earth woman looked at Gamora seriously, nodded, and raised his hands.

Before Gamora could do anything rash, Peter jumped in. "I get it, Gamora. We are in trouble. I'm not saying we're not. I'm just trying to keep things light here while we figure out a plan of action. A plan which I have already figured out," Peter said, smiling.

Rocket rolled his eyes. "This oughta be good. What's your plan, hotshot?"

"We call the Nova Corps," Peter said, still smiling. The other members of the Guardians looked at him without saying a word. Peter waited for a response. *Any* response. Nothing.

Finally: "I am Groot."

Rocket shifted uncomfortably in his seat, and looked at Gamora, who looked at Drax, who looked at Peter. "That's actually…"

"Not a horrible idea," finished Gamora.

"Yes, now that we are allies, the Nova Corps could be helpful in this situation," Drax allowed.

Peter clapped his hands together, satisfied. "Great! Rocket, call the Nova Corps!"

* * *

To everyone's surprise, the Nova Corps arrived and towed the *Milano* to the nearest planet—an artificial construct known as the Tradepost. Repairs were made, and the *Milano* was back in business.

"Surprised to see you made the trip out just to see us," Peter said to Rhomann Dey. Dey was a member of the Nova Corps. Following the Battle of Xandar, he had been promoted to the

rank of Denarian. That was a high honor for a member of the Nova Corps.

"I'm not here just to see you, Star-Prince," Dey volleyed. "I'm here because your ship was attacked."

Peter held up a finger. "First of all, it's Star-Lord," he said, "and second, we were attacked?"

Dey nodded.

"That thing that hit our ship, it was a meteorite or a—"

Dey touched a button on his wrist gauntlet. A hologram hovered above it. "It wasn't a meteorite. It was one of these," Dey said, motioning his head at the hologram. They stared at an amorphous blob of some kind, something like an enormous amoeba that pulsed and moved with a mind of its own. It would routinely contract, then expand almost as if it was breathing. Almost as if it was alive.

"What is that ugly-looking thing?" Rocket asked, walking over to Dey and Peter.

"That's your mother," said Peter.

Dey rolled his eyes, trying to keep his composure and his companions on track. "That," he said loudly, grabbing everyone's attention, "is a very big problem."

"What is it with problems today? That's all I'm hearing. Gamora—'We've got a problem.' You—'We've got a problem,'" Peter rambled. "Rocket didn't say he has a problem but we all know he does, and Drax is Drax so there's that, and..."

Rhomann Dey sighed and shook his head. "The universe it not out to get you, Quill," he said. "I know your ego says

otherwise, but it's not. These things, however…" Dey looked at the hologram hovering above his gauntlet.

"Yeah, these things," Peter said. "So what exactly are these things? Why are they a problem? You are seriously ruining my day right now."

"I am Groot." Peter turned to look at the sapling, who was standing next to Rocket.

"I don't know, pal," Rocket said. "Some people just don't appreciate it when the Nova Corps does something nice for them."

Peter rolled his eyes. "Really? You're lecturing me about gratitude? Do you really wanna go there? Because we can if you want to."

"You are both idiots," said Drax, hefting himself between Peter and Rocket. "Talk, Rhomann Dey. Tell us about this problem."

"We don't know what they're called. The thing that collided with the *Milano* and breached its hull is one of them. We've been getting reports from outlying sectors that groups of these… creatures have been seen, disrupting shipping routes."

Gamora stood back from the briefing, watching, listening. She stared at the hologram intently, her eyes never leaving it. Something about it was so bizarre, and yet so familiar. Had she seen this before? Her concentration was so intense that she failed to notice the strange figure in the shadows, staring at her and the other Guardians of the Galaxy. Watching. Waiting.

* * *

"…are both idiots," said the massive, tattooed warrior. "Talk, Rhomann Dey. Tell us about this problem."

Yes, tell them all about their little "problem," Rhomann Dey, thought the strange figure. *Whatever "problem" these so-called Guardians of the Galaxy are facing now will pale in comparison to the world of hurt I shall bring to them.*

The figure trained his eyes on each member of the Guardians, making sure that everyone was present. Quill. Rocket. Groot. Drax. Gamora. How he hated them all. How they would suffer. How they would die.

✳ ✳ ✳

An hour later.

Rhomann Dey had finished his briefing; Rocket had taken another swing at Peter; Groot had said, "I am Groot" a few more times; Drax lost his patience; and Gamora observed, patiently taking everything in.

"—I said, are you ready to go? The *Milano*'s ready. Ish."

Her concentration broken, Gamora turned, and saw Peter standing next to her.

"Do you remember when I said we have a problem?" Gamora asked as she and Peter walked down a corridor and into an enormous hangar. The rest of the Guardians were there, boarding the now-repaired *Milano*.

Peter rubbed the back of his neck with his hand. "Yeah, I do, but that's all anyone wants to talk about and Rhomann Dey just covered it all and—"

Gamora planted herself directly in front of Peter, blocking his path.

"That thing that attacked us, that thing Rhomann Dey showed you—I have encountered them before," Gamora warned.

"So...you know what to do? Like, how we can stop them?"

"No one knows that," said Gamora, "because they kill everything that crosses their path."

"Whoa. When you say 'everything,' that's, like, an exaggeration, right?" Peter asked Gamora. Now that she had his full attention, Gamora moved out of his way, and walked purposefully toward the waiting spacecraft.

"It's no exaggeration," Gamora said flatly. "I don't exaggerate." That was true. She didn't exaggerate. If she said she was going to do something, like say, punch someone in the face one thousand times, she was going to do it. A hot jet of exhaust vented from a side port on the *Milano*. Drax and Groot were already aboard. Rocket stood outside the ship, giving it a final once-over.

"Are you two gonna get in?" Rocket prodded. "Or are you just gonna dance around all day?"

* * *

Rhomann Dey watched as the *Milano* lifted off from the hangar, shaking his head. He turned away, his strides carrying him toward his own ship.

Rhomann Dey wasn't the only one watching. The strange figure who had been following Gamora gazed as the *Milano* rose slowly into the sky, then lurched forward, accelerating away

until it became a single tiny, bright light that vanished into the horizon.

Soon, he thought. *With the tracker in place, there is nowhere I cannot follow them. But I will need a ship....*

"You going to stand there forever?"

Rhomann Dey motioned to the strange figure, who was blocking his path from the hangar to Dey's own vessel.

"Excuse me," the strange figure said. "Please forgive my presence."

"'Please forgive my presence'?" Dey echoed. "I'm just asking you to move. Don't make a big deal out of it. Unless you want *me* to make a big deal out of it."

The strange figure moved aside, allowing Rhomann Dey to press ahead. *You just made my list, Rhomann Dey*, thought the strange figure, eyeing Dey's craft.

* * *

Peter Quill sat behind the *Milano*'s controls. "Listen up, everyone," Peter announced. Drax immediately raised his head and began looking upward. Peter stared at Drax and moved on.

"Gamora knows something about these creepy, crawly whatever-they-ares that Rocket let damage the *Milano*. Gamora?" Peter said, turning to his teammate.

Rocket grumbled and said, "I wasn't even piloting the ship when that happened, but who takes the blame?"

Gamora shot Rocket a look that shut him right up. "The creature that disabled our ship is Van'Lan."

"That's his name: 'Van'Lan'?" asked Peter. "Is that, like, a first name or a last name?"

Gamora shook her head. "*They* are Van'Lan. A collective. The individual creatures are part of a whole."

Rocket looked at Gamora. "Part of a whole what?"

"The Van'Lan seek out their own kind. When they come into contact, they join. They become bigger. Stronger. Faster. Deadlier."

Drax shifted his weight from one foot to the other. "I will destroy them with my own hands."

Gamora glared at her massive teammate. "You do not understand. They will seek one another out until they reach a critical mass. Then they will unleash destruction your mind can't possibly comprehend."

"Maybe Drax's mind can't comprehend it," Peter said, "but I'm pretty sure mine can. So the thing that smashed into the *Milano*, that was just one of these Van'Lan guys?"

Gamora nodded. "Just one. Had it been any more, we would not be here."

"That's rough," said Rocket.

"What is rough?" asked Drax. "These creatures—these Van'Lan—is their skin a coarse texture?"

Peter rolled his eyes again. "Guys, if Gamora says these things are no joke, then they are no joke."

"I can't believe I'm saying this, but Star-Lord is right," Gamora said, and Peter smiled at her like a kid who just got a gold star from a teacher. "These creatures are death. Make no mistake. And they must be stopped. Now."

* * *

A few days ago, give or take.

Yondu Udonta had seen better days. He would see better days ahead. But right now, he was depressed, a feeling to which he was unaccustomed and which he couldn't have named if he tried.

Propping up the bar at the Boot of Jemiah, Yondu looked at the glass in front of him. It was half-empty. Maybe it was half-full. Maybe he didn't care what it was. Yondu tipped the glass over, its contents spilling over the top of the bar. He watched the liquid run.

Not long ago, Yondu and his team of Ravagers had been in possession of the Orb, the rarest of rare artifacts. But nothing in the universe is permanent, and Peter Quill, his former protégé, pulled a switch at the last minute...leaving Yondu with no Orb, no rare artifact. Nothing to sell. Not good business for a Ravager.

There were a few threats to kill and such mixed in there somewhere, but Yondu had a fondness for Peter—one that he wouldn't talk about if it killed him.

"Yondu Udonta?" came a voice from behind. Yondu turned slowly around, expecting to see his first mate, Kraglin.

It was not Kraglin. It was a man, one whom Yondu couldn't quite place. He wasn't tall, but he wasn't short. He wasn't big, but he wasn't small. He wore a long, dark coat. He was average in all respects. Unremarkable.

"Ain't you got eyes?" Yondu said, turning back to the bar. "I'm having a drink here." Yondu waved his right hand at the tipped-over glass.

"I have eyes, and they see someone who might know where I can find Peter Quill," said the stranger.

Yondu's eyes widened, but he didn't turn around. He motioned to the bartender for another drink.

"What's *your* problem with Quill?" Yondu queried, without looking up. He tapped a single finger slowly, rhythmically, on the bar's surface.

"I owe him," said the stranger. "He owes me. Him and those...friends...of his, the Guardians of the Galaxy."

The bartender set down the drink in front of Yondu. He circled a finger around the rim. "What," Yondu responded, "makes you think I care?"

The stranger let out a bitter laugh. "I *know* you care. Quill was like a son to you, and—"

Yondu whirled around, showing something sharp in a holster strapped to his side. Then he whistled.

It became apparent that the "something" Yondu had grabbed was his Yaka Arrow, and it was now pointed directly at the strange figure's head. "I came here to have a drink," Yondu said through clenched teeth. "Seems to me like *you* came here to *die*."

"I came here because I need your help. To find Quill," said the stranger. "I can pay."

Yondu thought about that for a moment, then re-holstered his weapon. He turned back toward his fresh drink. He tipped that one over, too. "Talk," he told the stranger.

* * *

Fifteen minutes later and the stranger was gone. Just like that. A brief conversation, a slap on the stranger's back, an exchange of units, and the stranger was gone. Yondu ordered himself another drink. He didn't know exactly where Peter was—how

could he? "Best chance of finding him? Follow the Nova Corps. He's buddy-buddy with them now," Yondu had advised.

Why had he done that? Peter Quill was the closest thing to family that Yondu had. Ever since he arrived on Earth, taking a young Peter Quill into the stars to see his father. Except he didn't take him to his father. Yondu kept Peter by his side, teaching him the ways of the Ravagers. Though he never admitted it to Peter, Yondu really did think of him like his own son.

And his "son" had switched the Orb for a phony, and left Yondu with nothing. He could appreciate Peter's wits, his cleverness, of course. But it didn't make him any less mad. Maybe that was why he told the stranger. Or maybe he needed an excuse to get himself out of Knowhere and try living again.

* * *

The thing about space travel is, it's kind of boring. Seen one star, you've seen 'em all. Supernova? Yawn. On the other hand, traveling through space with a talking baby tree, whatever Rocket was, a fierce warrior, and a deadly assassin had its share of excitement. And frustration. Peter Quill knew all about that.

"I don't have to take orders from you, 'Star-Lord,'" said Rocket, walking away from Peter.

"Well, actually, you kind of do," Peter shot back. "Especially since we're getting ready to go to war or whatever."

Rocket whirled around. "Why are we even doing this? What business is it of ours? So what if some creatures want to destroy some stuff? That kinda thing happens every day!"

"Man, what is with you?" Peter asked. "It is our business,

according to Gamora." As if on cue, Gamora strode over to Peter and Rocket, forcing herself into the debate.

"There is no choice here, Rocket," Gamora said. Rocket's fur bristled at those words. "It is resist the Van'Lan, stop them here, now. Or we will never stop them. And civilizations will crumble."

Rocket threw up his hands and walked away.

"It's like I don't have any say in this at all!" he said, his voice trailing behind him.

* * *

"The *Milano*'s sensors are attuned to the Van'Lan's energy signature," Gamora said. On a screen before them, the Guardians saw an amorphous blob of pulsing energy, moving slowly in relation to a small, blinking blip. The blinking blip represented the *Milano*.

"How are we sure that thing is the Van'Lan?" asked Peter.

Gamora's eyes never left the screen. "Residual energy from the Van'Lan's collision with our ship," she said. "We're using that unique energy signature as a homing beacon. It can detect that signature wherever it may lie. It will lead us right to the Van'Lan."

"I am Groot," said the sapling.

"Exactly." Rocket snorted. "So we find 'em. Great. Then what? Aren't these things supposed to be all-powerful?"

Drax pointed a finger at his throat. "Finger on throat—"

"Means death, yeah, I know," finished Peter. He rolled his eyes.

Gamora looked at Drax and nodded. "He's right. When we

encounter the Van'Lan, we must destroy them. Every last one of them."

Rocket leaned back in his chair. "We're good at destroyin' things," he said. "So this should be a cakewalk."

"Why would you walk through cake?" Drax asked.

*　*　*

The small blip on the screen grew closer. It wasn't far now. The distance between the small blip and the strange figure's own ship was narrowing. The tracking device was working perfectly. He had overheard Quill's conversation. He knew of the Guardians' mission. He knew it was dangerous, and that the Guardians may not survive.

He was there to make absolutely certain they would not.

He had taken Yondu's advice days ago, and monitored the frequencies of the Nova Corps. When the Corps arrived to help the Guardians and headed to the Tradepost for repairs, the strange figure was there. He had gotten close, so close. He could have finished it right there. But the Nova Corps would have seen him. Perhaps stopped him. He couldn't allow that.

No, this way was much better, much cleaner. While the Guardians were busy, distracted, fighting an insane, intergalactic menace, the strange figure would deliver the killing blow. The grudge would be settled. Balance would be restored.

The strange figure noticed a smell. He looked at his coat. Yondu had spilled a drink on it.

*　*　*

An alarm whined in the *Milano*'s main cabin, and the Guardians stirred.

"What is that?" Peter shouted over the alarm.

"I don't know!" answered Gamora.

"I am Groot!" said Groot with an edge to his voice.

Rocket was at the controls, and pointed to the screen in front of him. The glowing blob they had been tracking was still there, but closer. Closer still was not one, but two glowing blobs.

Heading directly for the *Milano*.

"Incoming!" Rocket roared.

The words were barely out of Rocket's mouth when the attack started. A tendril of glowing, pulsing energy lashed out at the *Milano*'s port side, barely grazing its surface. Sparks flew. The thing had hardly made contact, but it caused power aboard the ship to cut out momentarily, before returning.

"The Van'Lan," said Gamora. "They must have sensed we were following."

"Can they do that?" asked Peter.

"Easily," Gamora responded. "We must have drawn their attention somehow."

Drax looked out the cockpit to see two pulsing blobs of glowing energy in the distance. "It does not matter," he said, drawing himself up. "I shall walk through them like cake."

"Cake is great," Peter said, manning a weapons station, "but we're going to need to stop these guys right now. Let 'em have it!" Peter pressed a button, and his tunes blared inside the *Milano*.

"Can you do *anything* without listening to this noise?" Rocket snarled.

"A—it's not noise," Peter replied curtly. "And secondly, those things are moving way too fast for me to get a bead on 'em."

The energy blobs—the Van'Lan—zigzagged in front of the *Milano*. Peter fired bursts at them, but the Van'Lan moved too quickly, easily evading the blasts.

"We are not walking through them like cake," Drax observed.

The Van'Lan circled, then lashed out at the *Milano* once again. Each blob released a long, glowing ribbon of energy toward the ship on either side. The *Milano* turned, rolled, and evaded both attacks.

Then the *Milano* fired.

And it connected with one of the Van'Lan.

If the Van'Lan were capable of screaming—if such a thing was possible—then that's exactly the sound the Van'Lan made as it caught the *Milano*'s fire.

"Did you see that?" said Peter, dancing in his seat. "I hit that glowing energy blobby thing!"

The blast hit the Van'Lan head-on, and the creature recoiled. It moved backward with incredible speed, away from the *Milano*, out of range of its weapons. Rocket looked at the scanner. The blob continued to move away, heading for the larger blob in the distance.

A second later, the remaining Van'Lan that had been attacking the ship fled.

They were alone once more. Well, relatively speaking.

* * *

Peter sat back in his quarters, his feet up on his bed. There was a sound by the door. Gamora.

"Here to congratulate me on my excellent blob-shooting skills?" Peter asked, smiling.

Gamora looked serious, then her features softened. A little. "That was good shooting," she said, standing in the doorway. "But that was just a test. The Van'Lan wanted to see what we were capable of doing. What harm we could inflict. Those two scouts are returning to the others."

"No problem. We just have to be faster, and make it to the group before they do," Peter said. "Rocket's on it. I would never tell him to his face that he's a good pilot, but he's a good pilot, and he'll get us there ahead of them."

"I hope you're right."

"I'm always right! I'm Star-Lord!" Peter smiled.

"We are doomed," Gamora replied, a thin smile curling along her lips.

* * *

Tracking the Guardians of the Galaxy was a surprisingly easy task, the strange figure thought. They brought chaos with them wherever they went. He observed as the Guardians engaged some strange, amorphous, luminescent creatures. He made sure that his own craft remained cloaked and far enough away to remain undetected.

He laughed. Not that it mattered. The Guardians were engaged in a firefight with the creatures, and would hardly notice one tiny spacecraft floating harmlessly in the distance.

Except the occupant of this one tiny spacecraft wasn't quite so harmless.

The strange figure laughed again. Soon he would set himself upon the Guardians. Wrongs would be righted. Only one would walk away.

It would not be the Guardians, he thought.

* * *

Yondu let out a loud laugh and slapped his knee. He was once again at the controls of his M-ship, and he had zeroed in on the tracking device he had planted on the stranger in the bar. It was easy. All he had to do was slap him on the back and the near-microscopic tracking device was in place.

He looks like the kind of moron who won't ever take off his jacket, Yondu thought.

This was exactly what he needed—something to take his mind off everything. He didn't like the stranger, not one bit. Yondu may have been angry with Peter, but he was the closest thing to family that he had. And if anyone was going to mess with Peter, it was going to be Yondu. He was certain of that.

The M-ship cruised along, and Yondu slowed when he saw the stranger's craft wink out of sight on his scanner.

Cloaking device. Strictly amateur hour.

Yondu laughed again. At least this made things interesting. That was when his scanners picked up another signal, dead ahead. Two amorphous blobs of some sort, attacking an unknown vessel.

No, not unknown.

The *Milano.*

Now this, Yondu thought, *is very, very interesting.* He pushed himself back in his seat and watched.

* * *

It was quiet aboard the *Milano.* The calm before the storm. The Guardians had to make it to the Van'Lan before the two scouts

could return and call an attack. Any other outcome would spell disaster. While Gamora, Peter, and Drax steeled themselves for the battle ahead, Groot approached his diminutive comrade. Rocket paced the halls of the *Milano*, which was new for him. Rocket was used to having energy to spare, but was never so nervous. What was wrong? What was different about this situation than any other?

"I am Groot."

"What's it to you?" Rocket said in a short, clipped tone. "So I'm a little moody, so what? A guy's allowed to be a little moody without having a tree come down on him, ain't he?"

"I am Groot."

Rocket let out a heavy sigh. He didn't have it in him to scream at Groot again. "Yeah, I know, I know. Look, I'm just wonderin' if this attack is such a good idea, is all!"

"I *am* Groot."

Rocket waved a hand at his friend. "I don't know! I don't know why I suddenly care! Maybe because the odds are freakin' terrible? Maybe because I just got you back? Maybe because I don't want to lose you again? Geez, look at me, havin' feelings." Rocket turned away from Groot. The small, treelike being put a gnarled twig on Rocket's shoulder.

"I am Groot."

"Thanks, pal. I needed that." Rocket looked at his friend, and smiled…just a little. Groot nodded.

"I am Groot."

"You're too young to be using language like that."

* * *

"How are we looking?" Peter asked Gamora. His fellow Guardian was monitoring the ship's scanner, tracking the movement of the two Van'Lan scouts, as well as their ultimate destination—the gathering collective of Van'Lan.

"The *Milano*'s engines are pushed to their limit," she said, not taking her eyes from the scanner. "We remain ahead of the scouts. For now."

Peter shifted in his seat uncomfortably. Drax stood above him.

"How long until we intercept the main group?" Peter asked.

"Given present speed? Less than an hour."

"Soon we do battle," Drax said, placing an enormous hand on Peter's shoulder.

"*Buckle up!* Things are about to go haywire!" Peter yelled to the crew of the *Milano*.

"What do you mean, 'about to'?" Rocket asked, grabbing on to a console as the ship was buffeted back and forth.

"I am Groot!" said the sapling, with an urgency in his tone.

"We're under attack by giant, floating blob-things from hell!" Rocket replied, venom in his voice.

Drax and Gamora looked out the cockpit to see the source of the attack.

The Van'Lan. Each of the creatures moved independently of the other, forming a massive swarm blocking the *Milano*'s path.

"According to the scanner, they shouldn't be here," said Gamora breathlessly. "We're still an hour away!"

"The scanner lies," said Drax.

Peter ran up to Drax and Gamora. For once, his expression

looked serious. Well, serious for him. It was kind of hard to tell, to be honest.

"These space blobs are smarter than we thought," said Peter. "They fooled the scanners somehow."

Gamora looked at Peter. "That seems obvious."

Peter tipped his head slightly. "Are you…are you messing with me? I can never tell, but it seems like you might be, and—"

ZZZZZZRRRRRAAAAAKKKKK!

Something collided with the *Milano*'s starboard side, causing a shower of sparks to rain inside the ship. Rocket caught the brunt of it, and a small patch of fur started to smolder. With great care and speed, Groot patted the spot, putting out the tiny spark.

"Thanks, pal! Geez, it figures only the guy with fur would get hit," Rocket fumed.

"Rocket!" Peter shouted. "Who's flying the ship?!"

Rocket and Peter looked at each other momentarily.

They both raced back to the pilot's seat.

* * *

Peter weaved the ship and ducked through the onslaught. The Van'Lan first tried to attack individually, sending various glowing blobs of energy to lash out at the *Milano*. Ribbons of energy issued forth, rippling through space, missing the ship by mere millimeters.

Peter was the absolute dictionary definition of concentration as he used all his piloting skill to evade the enemy.

"They don't seem to know how to handle all this fancy

flying," Peter said, allowing himself a little satisfaction over his efforts. "Let's bring the attack to them now!"

"I will not bring them an attack," said Drax, a smile forming on his face that was downright disturbing. "I will bring them nothing. I will simply attack, and they will perish."

"That was a—"

"Metaphor," Drax said, his downright disturbing smile even more downright disturbing, somehow. "Yes, I know. I like your metaphors, Peter. They amuse me."

"Stop talking! We need to end this, now!" shouted Gamora. At that, everyone snapped to, and Rocket manned the *Milano*'s weapons station. As Peter expertly ran the gauntlet of Van'Lan, Rocket unleashed a barrage of bursts at the creatures. Every shot landed.

"Every shot landed!" Rocket yelled, whooping from his seat. "Every shot! Have you ever seen better shooting than tha—?"

ZZZZARRRRAAAKKKK!!!

A brilliant tendril of energy thrashed across the *Milano*'s cockpit, causing the craft to spin in a circle while at the same time moving forward. Sparks rained inside the vessel, and the crew held on as the craft continued to spin.

They started to feel pretty nauseated. Because of the spinning.

Rocket spat. "I'm gonna lose my lunch!" But he was spared that because—

ZARRRRKKAAAAAAKKK!!!

Another attack from the Van'Lan, this one clipping the ship's tail. More sparks. Peter felt the controls go slack for a moment,

then recover. But one good thing did come out of this latest blow: The ship stopped spinning.

✳ ✳ ✳

Look at them, thought the strange figure. *Fighting for their lives against an unknown enemy.*

While he enjoyed watching the Guardians suffer, he knew that to have them perish at the hands of this unknown enemy would rob him of his ultimate revenge. And that, he couldn't have. As much as he hated to admit it, the strange figure would have to help the Guardians of the Galaxy.

I might be sick, he thought.

✳ ✳ ✳

The *Milano* continued to duck and weave through the volley of Van'Lan attacks. It was some of the best piloting Peter Quill had ever done. Even Rocket could admit that, though never to Peter, never out loud, never ever, ever.

However, the ceaseless attacks were taking their toll. Yes, Peter had done an expert job keeping the ship and his teammates out of harm's way, for the most part. But even the stray glances were doing their fair share of damage to the *Milano*'s spaceworthiness. In other words, no matter how well Peter flew, sooner or later, the *Milano* was going down.

"I'm doing everything I can!" Peter shouted to no one in particular. "But expert piloting by an expert pilot, which is me, is only going to get us so far!"

Gamora looked out the cockpit to see the Van'Lan circling, getting ready for another attack. "Drax. With me. We take

the battle to them," she said with determination. "Peter. Stop the ship."

Peter paused, then slowly turned his head toward Gamora. "It sounded an awful lot like you said the ship needs to stop, which means we'll be a sitting duck."

Gamora nodded. "Exactly. We need to appear damaged beyond repair. To draw the Van'Lan in. For what Drax and I will do."

Drax smiled, drawing his twin knives.

* * *

Moments later, after a particularly close call with one of the Van'Lan, Peter entered a sequence on his screen to release countermeasures, which appeared to be debris from an explosion. The debris drifted away, and Peter let the *Milano* come to a dead, drifting stop in space. To all outward eyes, it appeared that the *Milano* had been hit, damaged beyond repair, and was now dead in space.

As the *Milano* drifted, a strange thing happened. The Van'Lan slowly took formation in a way they had not before. They formed a circle, which began to rotate slowly around the *Milano*'s perimeter. Steadily, the perimeter drew closer and closer, the Van'Lan growing nearer and nearer toward the (apparently) incapacitated ship.

The Guardians waited.

The Van'Lan drew nearer.

The Guardians waited some more.

Closer.

And *that* is precisely when everything went truly haywire.

It's impossible to say what the Van'Lan were or were not prepared for. As a species, they were unlike anything that had been encountered. Their thought processes were unknown. Were they even actually alive?

These questions were all unanswerable.

What could be answered, known, and quantified was this: The *Milano* appeared to be a lifeless husk, and the Van'Lan appeared very eager to destroy it.

As the Van'Lan drew closer to the apparently derelict ship, circling, the blobs of light seemed to merge together. They weren't yet one massive whole, but tendrils of energy from each reached out to the others. As if pooling their energies, their consciousness.

"We will walk through you like cake!"

* * *

Drax.

FZZZZZZZZZTTTTTT!

Drax, with a very large energy blaster. Leveled squarely at the Van'Lan. Causing capital-*D* damage.

FZZZZZZZZZTTTTTT!!!

Gamora.

Gamora, with an equally large energy blaster. Leveled squarely at the Van'Lan. Causing capital-*D* damage.

Just as the Van'Lan had been about to join together and annihilate the *Milano*, Drax and Gamora appeared. They came from the *Milano*'s hatch in life-support suits.

The energy blasts hit the Van'Lan, and the glowing

blobs emitted high-pitched squeals. Screams? Who could say? Immediately, the Van'Lan began to scramble, their tendrils retracting from one another. They ceased circling the *Milano.*

"They're backing off!" Gamora said. "Blast them into oblivion!"

FZZZZZZZZTTTTTT!!! FZZZZZZZZZTTTTTT!!!

The energy blasts found their target once more, and the Van'Lan recoiled, pulsing, squealing. At least one of their number began to react strangely, as if it were dissipating. It looked like someone had dropped a bead of dye into a glass of water, the color slowly ebbing away as it mingled with the water.

Which is exactly what happened to that Van'Lan. It appeared to struggle to keep its essence together, but another blast from Drax's weapon fractured it even further. Energy began to bleed from its form out into space, and soon, that Van'Lan ceased to exist.

✷ ✷ ✷

From afar, the strange figure watched the battle, undetected, as the pulsing energy creatures attacked the *Milano.* He rubbed his hands together anxiously.

Now, while they least expect it, he thought. *While their attention, their resources are stretched thin, and they fight for their lives.*

Now, he thought to himself, *I will have my revenge. I will strike. And the Guardians of the Galaxy will be no more.*

✷ ✷ ✷

It was the perfect shot. Too perfect. There was no challenge to it, in fact. The target sat there, immobile, drifting, powerless.

While a battle waged, the vessel appeared unmoving, just lying in wait. He saw Gamora and Drax in the vacuum of space, fighting valiantly against the strange, glowing creatures. Amazingly, and against all odds, they were winning, beating them back, turning the tide.

And still, the vessel didn't move. Just watching. Waiting. For something.

Yondu Udonta couldn't stand the suspense any longer, and he fired.

Not at the *Milano*, but at a cloaked ship not too far from Peter Quill's beloved ship.

"That's what you get for makin' me spill my drink," Yondu said with a laugh as he watched the tiny ship spiral out of control.

* * *

Inside the Milano.

While Drax and Gamora wielded their weapons outside the ship, slowly but surely chipping away at the Van'Lan, Rocket, Peter, and Groot had their hands full. They sat at a console, monitoring a data feed from their comrades' weapons.

"You gotta dial it up, Groot! Up the frequency, now!" bellowed Rocket.

"I am Groot!" replied the sapling.

Groot entered a sequence into the console, which remotely changed the frequency of Drax's and Gamora's energy weapons. By feeding the energy signature into the ship's computers, they

were able to generate an ever-changing sequence of energy frequencies designed to disrupt the Van'Lan, and do maximum damage.

"Take that, ya blob," said Rocket, satisfied.

Peter was watching his console intently, eyes glued to the readouts.

"Rocket," he said with a sense of urgency, "what do a whole bunch of zeroes in a row mean?"

Rocket looked up at Peter and scratched his head. "A whole bunch of zeroes? That means the weapons are just about out of power, but that can't happen because—"

A warning sound blared from the computer.

*　*　*

Outside the ship, Drax and Gamora were fighting the Van'Lan, and winning. The energy creatures were falling back, seemingly afraid of the effects of the Guardians' weapons.

The weapons that suddenly stopped working.

"Quill!" Gamora shouted into her comm unit. "We have a problem! Fix it!"

Rocket and Peter were at each other's throats. There were punches, kicks, and insults. *"I. Am. Groot!"* thundered a voice, much deeper than one would think capable of coming from such a tiny tree. It got both Rocket's and Peter's attention.

"He's right," Rocket said, releasing Peter from his clutches. "It's not your fault; it's not my fault; it doesn't matter. We just gotta fix this. Or people are gonna die."

"I got an idea," Peter said. "Maybe we don't need the weapons to beat the Van'Lan. Maybe we just need the ship."

"That…sounds ridiculous," Rocket said, shaking his head. "Let's do it."

✳ ✳ ✳

His weapon no longer working, Drax hurled the dead object at the Van'Lan. Gamora simply let her weapon drift, and she motioned for Drax to head back inside the *Milano*.

Drax ignored her, drew both his knives, and approached the nearest Van'Lan.

"He is stubborn, stupid, and undeniably brave," Gamora said to herself. "He's also going to get himself—"

Drax slashed at the Van'Lan. The blade connected, spewing a trail of energy into the ether of space.

"—not killed," said Gamora.

"Gamora!"

Star-Lord's voice, over the comm unit.

"Peter!" she responded.

"Grab Drax and get inside—now! We're gonna try something!"

Now we're in trouble, Gamora thought. She lunged forward, drifting over to Drax, and grabbed his arm. The warrior turned and glared at her. She said nothing, but motioned with her head toward the *Milano*'s hatch. The look on her face said it all. Go. Now.

Despite his warrior's instinct, Drax followed Gamora, and they retreated to the safety of the *Milano*.

"We're inside!" Gamora said, the hatch closing behind her.

"Now! *Now!*" Peter Quill shouted.

"I am Groot!"

"Gotcha!"

Peter, Groot, and Rocket entered the sequence into their respective consoles. The sequence brought the *Milano*'s engines to life.

The Van'Lan, no longer threatened by the energy weapons, drew closer.

"Hit the deck and don't open your eyes!" Peter Quill shouted.

There was a brilliant burst of light from the engines.

The darkness of space turned white.

It seemed to stay that way forever. Slowly, inexorably, the white faded, and the familiar dark emptiness of space returned.

Empty. Void of Van'Lan. They were no more.

"That," said Drax, "was a walk through cake."

*　*　*

It was all Peter's idea. Using the Van'Lan's energy signature, they programmed the *Milano*'s engines to disperse the same frequencies as Drax's and Gamora's energy weapons. The result? A sudden, instantaneous burst of unheard-of energy, directed outward, with a frequency that dispelled the Van'Lan.

A brilliant idea, if Star-Lord did say so himself. (He did.) But one that cost the Guardians dearly. Once again, their spacecraft was rendered inert, lifeless.

Once again, the Guardians of the Galaxy were in need of a cosmic tow truck.

An hour later, the Nova Corps arrived.

*　*　*

"That boy is good," said Yondu as he watched the action from his M-ship. A Nova Corps vessel brought the *Milano* behind it,

and headed for the Tradepost. A part of him wanted to follow, to congratulate Peter on his hard-earned victory.

Maybe kill him.

Yondu laughed. Not today. The Guardians of the Galaxy might have a free pass with the Nova Corps these days, but Yondu Udonta did not. Best to leave well enough alone—for now. Besides, it was enough that Yondu got to take a shot at that long-jacket-wearing stranger who had bothered him back at the Boot of Jemiah.

"I wonder what's gonna happen to that guy," he said, chuckling.

* * *

Back at the Tradepost, the Guardians headed to the nearest watering hole while they waited for the *Milano* to be repaired once more.

"Star-Lord!"

Peter turned his head to see Rhomann Dey approaching. He had with him a strange-looking man who wore a long coat. He couldn't place the man. Unremarkable.

"Rhomann Dey," said Peter. "Thanks for the lift. Again. Hey, who's your friend here?"

"I am your death, Peter Quill!" spat the strange figure.

"This guy is a problem, is who he is," Dey responded. "He stole my ship! Can you believe it? Took it for a little joyride. Apparently had a little problem out in space. Someone took a shot at him, knocked out the engine. We brought him in same time we got you."

Peter nodded. "I'm curious, though," he said, looking directly at the strange figure. "Why are you my death?"

The strange figure glowered. "You really don't know, do you? Don't know how you ruined me?"

Peter stared, his eyes darting around, as if trying to remember. He shook his head no.

"Who is *this*, Rhomann Dey?" said Gamora dismissively.

"The Boot of Jemiah! The Orloni races!" the strange figure whined. The Orloni were small rodent-like creatures. The races pitted these animals against a hungry, reptilian beast called the F'Saki. People bet on the races for units.

"This is literally ringing no bells," Peter said, scratching his head.

"You and your idiot friends interrupted the Orloni races with your ridiculous quarreling! I was winning! I could have won! I lost all my units"

"Wait," said Peter. "So you were going to kill us…"

"Yes!"

"…because you lost units…"

"*Yes!*"

"…on a game?" Peter finished.

The strange figure was hopping mad now. "I *tried* to kill you! I was *this* close to blowing you out of the stars!"

"But someone blew you out of the stars first," Dey interjected.

The strange figure fumed.

"This has been the weirdest day," said Peter Quill, as the strange figure was led away, still hungry for revenge that would never come.

* * *

"Well, we've got time to kill," said Peter as the Guardians waited for the repairs to the *Milano*.

"We have killed enough today," Drax replied. "Let us enjoy life for the moment."

Peter smiled. "I'm gonna take that as a joke, so well done, Drax."

"I am Groot."

"You said it, pal," Rocket added. "We owe ourselves a little R 'n' R."

Gamora smiled at Peter. "You did well, Star-Lord. I'm impressed."

Rocket rolled his eyes. "Okay, that's it. Drax, Groot, with me. Let's get a drink and leave these two to tell each other how great they are."

The three other Guardians walked off to a club in the distance. Peter and Gamora watched them leave.

"Were you really impressed?" Peter asked Gamora.

Gamora looked at Peter, and placed a hand on his shoulder.

"No," she said softly. "I just wanted to get the others to leave."

Peter Quill laughed, and all was right in the galaxy.

For a minute, at least.